Fiddle Dee Death

John F. Blair, Publisher
Winston-Salem, North Carolina

Fiddle Dee Death

Caroline Cousins

Published by John F. Blair, Publisher

*The paper in this book meets the guidelines
for permanence and durability of the
Committee on Production Guidelines for
Book Longevity of the Council on Library Resources*

*Cover photograph courtesy of
South Carolina Film Commission*

Library of Congress Cataloging-in-Publication Data

Cousins, Caroline.
Fiddle dee death / by Caroline Cousins.
p. cm.
ISBN 0-89587-286-2 (hardcover : alk. paper)
ISBN 0-89587-275-7 (paperback : alk. paper)
1. Southern States—Fiction. 2. Scandals—Fiction. I. Title.
PS3603.0857F53 2003
813'.6—dc21
2003004452

Printed in Canada

For the family

prologue

On the longest night of the year, the old house slumbers. Moonlight silvers the roof and silhouettes the ancient sheltering oaks and tall pines against a star-studded sky.

A clear night. A calm night. But not a completely silent one. Wavelets lap at the dock reaching into the river governed by the tides of the nearby ocean; an owl hoots; small animals scurry in the underbrush for safety; inside the house, a board creaks as if drawing in from the cold. There will be frost by morning.

A small light suddenly winks on in an upper window, almost like a reflection from a passing car. But the main road is two curving, tree-lined miles away, and no car is crunching up the oyster-shell drive this late.

The light moves and flickers. It looks like a candle, or maybe just a flashlight held by an unsteady hand. The light holds still for a moment, then vanishes as suddenly as it appeared. And the house is dark again.

chapter one

Dad-Gum, He's Dead

At exactly five o'clock in the afternoon, the double mahogany doors opened wide.

"Welcome to Pinckney Plantation."

It took me a moment to realize the startling vision in purple Scarlett O'Hara get-up ushering us into the plantation house's entry hall was my very own first cousin once removed, Cecelia Lynn Matthews, better known as Cissy.

"What do you think?" asked Margaret Ann, gazing fondly at her sixteen-year-old daughter. "I made it myself. Doesn't she look a picture?"

"Of what? An escapee from Tara World?" I whispered back. "Did you tear down the curtains from the Episcopal church social hall?"

"No, silly. Miss Augusta got the material on sale at Wal-Mart in

Charleston. Do you think the parasol is too much? That was her idea, too. Thought it might bring in more tourists."

I thought the whole thing was too much, but I kept my mouth shut. There's no talking with Margaret Ann without getting into some big, long discussion. I should know. That was how I'd ended up here in this drafty old house two days after Christmas. I had been perfectly comfortable on the couch at my folks' when Margaret Ann breezed in without so much as a howdy-do and told me to get a move on, we were going to Pinckney to catch Cissy's last tour and give her a ride home.

"But I'm working," I'd protested.

"No, you're not," my cousin said, opening the tins on the kitchen counter to see if any of Mama's bourbon balls were left. "You're just lying there."

"Am not. Peaches and I are thinking up my next story for *Perfect Pet*. Aren't we, Peaches?"

The big orange cat didn't answer, not that Margaret Ann would have heard. She was too busy rattling tins and rattling on about how she bet I hadn't been out of the house all day, since I'd waved off both sets of our parents that morning on their way to Charleston to catch a New Year's cruise to the Caribbean.

"I walked to the beach," I said.

This hardly counted, since the Atlantic Ocean—or at least the St. Helena Sound part of it—was only a couple of dunes from Mama and Daddy's front porch. Full moons and high tides and it's practically to the steps.

"Oh, do," said Margaret Ann. "Time's a-wastin', and you've hardly seen Aunt Cora, and I expect she'll be there, 'cause all those state historical-society people were coming today from Charleston as part of that conference."

But looking around Pinckney's wallpapered hallway now, I didn't spot our great-aunt among the dozen or so tourists listening to Cissy's spiel about how Pinckney Plantation was the pride of Indigo Island.

"Indigo was settled in the 1700s by British colonists," she said in a confident tour-guide tone that combined those of a news anchor and a kindergarten teacher. "The colonists hoped to grow rice like their neighbors on other coastal islands to the north, but they soon found that indigo—the plant used for its distinctive blue-purple dye—was a better cash crop." She twirled her frilly parasol and used it to point at her full skirt. "My dress is what we call Pinckney purple, a variation on the more traditional blue indigo."

This was the first I'd heard of Pinckney purple. Must be Miss Augusta's way of rationalizing her Wal-Mart purchase.

Cissy continued. "After sea-island cotton was introduced, the planters found it was even more lucrative than indigo. Several of them made small fortunes and began building fine homes like this one on Magnolia Bluff." She smiled prettily, showing off the white, even teeth that had cost her parents a small fortune. "This is the second house on this site," Cissy explained. "The first one burned in 1840, but the chimney you'll see in the front parlor is part of the original structure."

Cissy didn't go into much detail about Indigo itself, which is snuggled up against its big sister, Edisto Island, along the coast of the South Carolina Low Country between Beaufort and Charleston. Anyone who makes the turn off Highway 17 and crosses the drawbridge over the Intracoastal Waterway down from the Dawhoo Cut ends up on Indigo. That's the only way onto the island, unless you come by boat. Most islanders—the several hundred who live on Indigo year-round and a couple thousand more who have weekend or summer houses—are scared to death the barrier island will be discovered and developed. In a word, ruined. Tourists are welcome for short visits, the emphasis being on *short*.

"You are now standing in the long hallway that runs the length of the house," Cissy said. "It allows the breeze to flow through in the hot summer afternoons. The front of the house originally faced the waterway, which was the main mode of transportation. The kitchen was located in a separate building because of the fire hazard."

Margaret Ann and I yawned simultaneously, then had to stifle our giggles. We'd both been tour guides at Pinckney during high school, when Miss Augusta had first opened the downstairs to the public, and except for Pinckney purple, it didn't seem like she'd changed a word of the script in the twenty years since then.

"We will now go into the formal dining room," Cissy said. "Remember to stay behind the ropes. And please, no flash photography or video cameras."

That last part was new. I tugged on Margaret Ann's suede jacket, and we ducked behind the group Cissy was shepherding and went down the long hall to the new kitchen, where the tourists weren't allowed. It would be awhile before Cissy and her entourage made their way through the house and she turned them loose on the landscaped grounds.

"Hey, Jimmy," Margaret Ann said to the lanky teenager leaning against the back door and looking out at the darkening day and the moss-draped oaks still dripping from the afternoon's rain. "Thought you were hunting today. Did you come to get Cissy?"

"Yes, ma'am," he said.

I smiled. Margaret Ann's nickname since forever has been Mam, on account of her initials. She was a Mikell before she married a Matthews. I started to say something, but as usual, Margaret Ann was there before me.

"This is my cousin Lindsey Fox. She belongs to Aunt Mary Ann and Uncle Lee."

I couldn't even get out a hello because Margaret Ann was talking a mile a minute, trying to explain the intertwining branches of our family tree, telling him how we're more than first cousins, 'cause our mamas are sisters and our daddies are first cousins.

"We have the same grandparents on one side and the same great-grandparents on both sides," she concluded. "But we're not double first cousins. More like one and a half."

It still made us sound like something out of *Deliverance*. But Jimmy just nodded. He and Cissy had been seeing each other a couple of months now, from what Cissy had told me over Christmas dinner, so he was probably used to Margaret Ann's monologues, which are actually pretty entertaining, as long as you don't want to get a word in edgewise and can follow her conversational leaps.

"Have you seen Aunt Cora?" she asked. "And where's Miss Augusta? I thought Marietta would be here."

I was looking forward to seeing Marietta Manigault, Miss Augusta's longtime housekeeper, famous for her feather-light biscuits and feathered Sunday hats.

"Marietta was, but she left right after I came in," Jimmy said. "She heard an owl hoot and mumbled something about it being a bad omen, and about getting home before dark."

"Marietta thinks everything's a bad omen these days," Margaret Ann said. "Ever since Miss Augusta took her to that historical-society meeting to hear about Gullah superstitions, she's been talking about haints and evil eyes. She never did that when Lindsey and I were in high school. Back then, she talked about how black was beautiful, and maybe how she'd wear her hair in an Afro. But she's still got that bun."

Margaret Ann opened the refrigerator and stuck her head inside. I could hear her voice but not what she was saying.

"Do y'all want some of this Coke or not?" she asked, emerging with an almost-full plastic bottle. "I don't think it's gone flat yet." She gave it a couple of vigorous shakes, just in case.

"Maybe you better open it over the sink," I said, backing across the room.

"There," Margaret Ann said, pouring the fizzy liquid into three jelly jars. "I tried to interview her for my oral-history project in college, and she said, 'Don't they have anything better to teach you than bothering old folks?' No, if you ask me, I think both Marietta and Miss Augusta are getting funnier the older they get."

I knew she meant funny peculiar, not funny ha-ha. "They're both in their eighties, 'cause Aunt Cora's right up there with them." I turned to Jimmy. "You didn't see Aunt Cora?"

"No, ma'am."

He did have nice manners. Good looks, too, and no obvious body piercings. It would be interesting to see how long he and Cissy lasted. Her daddy, J. T., says she changes boyfriends more often than he does the oil in his pickup.

"I think she and Miss Augusta went with the historic people back to the museum," Jimmy volunteered. "Cissy said their bus back to Charleston was supposed to leave at five."

So much for seeing Aunt Cora, although I was sure I'd see plenty of her the next couple weeks, while I was house-sitting because my duplex in Charlotte was being replumbed. Our parents' last instructions had been for Margaret Ann and me to keep an eye on Aunt Cora, who has always been like another grandmother to us.

"Why do you suppose they had this conference so close to Christmas?" I asked Mam. "You'd think it would be a bad time."

"Maybe not. Probably a bunch of them are connected with schools or colleges, and now's when they're on vacation. And it's not like there's anything much going on except after-Christmas sales, unless you're going to the Gator Bowl or the Peach Bowl. Look at us. We don't have anything to do till New Year's Eve."

This was true. I was looking forward to some peace and quiet after all the pre-Christmas hubbub. I had no immediate deadlines, just a stack of books I wanted to read.

"Hey," said Cissy, coming into the kitchen and hanging the ruffled parasol on a hook on the pantry door. "I didn't know y'all were still here. But Mama, look. I think you hemmed this dress too short. I heard some people snickering when I was standing on the stairs."

I refrained from comment, but it was true that you could see Cissy's white Nikes peeping from beneath the lilac petticoat trim. Purple actually flattered her, bringing out the blue in the large eyes she inherited from J. T.

"I'll fix it tonight," Margaret Ann said. "I guess we'll go on, since Jimmy's here to carry you home. Just let me rinse these and stick 'em in the dishwasher." I quickly finished my Coke before she could take it, then handed over the glass. "Dinner's at seven, just leftovers, but there's plenty, so you plan on staying, too, Jimmy. And since Marietta's gone and so's Miss Augusta, go ahead and lock up."

"Miss Augusta's not here?" Cissy said. "But I thought I heard her upstairs awhile ago. There was a big thud up above the parlor."

"Heavens, maybe she's hurt herself."

Margaret Ann headed to the back stairs to the second floor, where Miss Augusta lives when she's on the island. It's always been off-limits to visitors. We'd sneaked up there years ago, but Cissy had told us the door at the top was kept locked now, for insurance purposes.

"Miss Augusta, are you there?" yelled Margaret Ann in a voice loud enough to wake the dead, or the deaf. Miss Augusta's hard of hearing and sometimes turns off her hearing aid when there are tours downstairs. "It's me, Margaret Ann, and I've got Lindsey with me. Miss Augusta, are you there? I'm coming up."

"Me, too," I said. "Maybe we'll see the ghost."

"What ghost?" Jimmy asked.

"The ghost of Pinckney Plantation," Cissy said. "We wanted to put her in the tour, but Miss Augusta won't let us."

"She wouldn't let us either," I said.

"Cissy, you can tell ghost stories later," Margaret Ann said. "Right now, I need you and Jimmy to go outside and see if you see Miss Augusta's Caddy or any other cars. Lindsey, come on."

The entryway was in shadows and the steep stairs so dark you couldn't even tell if the door at the top was open, much less locked. Margaret Ann hesitated.

"For goodness' sake," I said, reaching over her shoulder to turn on the stairway light.

The bulb was so dim—or covered with dust—that we could hardly see going up the narrow stairs single-file.

"The door's open," Margaret Ann said, stopping so suddenly I pitched into her back. "Here, you go first. Age before beauty."

She has never let me forget that I'm all of two days older than she is. "When somebody said that to Dorothy Parker," I told her, "she said, 'Pearls before swine.' "

I swept in front of Mam before she could answer back and flipped on another light. It cast even more shadows down the long hall, which had rooms facing each other on either side. The whole place smelled of mildew and mice, with mothballs mixed in.

Margaret Ann opened a door to a room empty of everything but an iron bedstead, its blue-tick mattress rolled and tied at one end. "This place is giving me the creeps," she said.

"It is kind of spooky up here." I stopped short when lumpy white figures loomed out of the dark room across the hall. "Look at this. The furniture's all shrouded in sheets. It's like Miss Havisham's."

"Was she in *Wuthering Heights*?"

"No, dummy. *Great Expectations*. We had to read it in school. Miss Fishburne's class."

"Oh, I remember. But I don't think I ever read it. Just saw the movie."

"I think Miss Augusta must have moved some stuff to the third floor. I remember this room as being more crowded."

By now, we were in the second-floor parlor next to Miss Augusta's bedroom. There wasn't anyone in either room, just some serviceable mahogany furniture and a couple of Oriental rugs that had seen better days. There were also enough cobwebs in the corners to decorate for Halloween.

"Marietta must not come up here," I said. "You'd think as persnickety as Miss Augusta is, she'd have this place all spit and polish."

"She only cares that the downstairs looks good for the tourists.

Her townhouse in Charleston is real nice. She had a decorator."

"Do you remember how to get upstairs to the attic?"

"There's stairs in a closet in one of the rooms. Sort of like a Nancy Drew mystery. Wasn't there one called *The Hidden Staircase*?"

"I think so," I said. "There was one about an old clock, and something about a bungalow. I didn't know what that was then. I thought it was some sort of an animal, like a big rat or a wolverine."

I opened the parlor closet door. It held only some cardboard boxes and a few empty wire hangers. "Nothing here."

"I gave away all our Nancy Drew books after Cissy got too old for them. Wish now I'd kept them." Margaret Ann peered behind the fireplace screen. "Nothing here either. I bet some of those books might be worth something now. A bunch of them were the ones Bonnie and I had when we were little, and I think there were even one or two that might have been our mamas'."

"I remember wanting a roadster," I said. "It sounded so much more sophisticated than a car."

I was in Miss Augusta's bathroom. A can of Aqua Net was perched on the pedestal sink next to a pink toothbrush in a glass. The claw-foot tub was empty except for a rubber mat.

"What was the name of Nancy Drew's boyfriend?" Margaret Ann's voice carried across the hall. "Ed? Fred?"

"Ned," I said automatically. "Like in dead."

Margaret Ann didn't laugh. In fact, she didn't say anything.

"Mam? You okay?"

I found her standing beside a closet she'd opened next to an age-darkened wardrobe. My eyes followed hers to the hardwood floor in front of her.

"I think we better call 911 and tell them someone's hurt,"

Margaret Ann said. Her voice was as small as I'd ever heard it.

I took a deep breath. "I don't think he's hurt," I said, trying to look at her and not at the twisted figure face-down at the bottom of the attic stairs. "I think he's dead."

"How do you know he's not just unconscious?" Margaret Ann sounded more like herself. "How many dead bodies have you seen outside of a funeral parlor?"

"Too many," I said. "You forget that I covered cops that year I worked at the TV station."

"You don't know for sure. We ought to see if he's breathing. Maybe he's just paralyzed."

"If he is, he's not going to appreciate your messing with his head."

Margaret Ann knelt beside the man. "I know better than to touch his head. All the blood seems to be under his face, though. There's not any on the back near that bald spot. I'm going to see if he's got a pulse on his arm."

My stomach was starting to feel funny. One of the main reasons I'd quit the TV station in Charlotte was because of all the crime scenes and wrecks I'd had to cover. I knew what a shotgun blast could do to a man's face, and what someone looked like with a knife stuck in his throat. The worst, though, were the fires and drownings that left people not even looking like people. This man didn't look so bad, except for the blood pooled under him. Margaret Ann would have to point that out, knowing how squeamish I am. She's not. After raising a tomboy, having a husband who hunts and fishes, and delivering who knew how many litters of puppies, she wasn't going to be bothered by the sight of some blood.

"Head wounds bleed a lot," I said. My stomach gave a lurch. I have to close my eyes to clean up Peaches' hairballs, and I've been known to leave a room rather than step on a palmetto bug.

"I don't feel anything," Margaret Ann said, "but I may not be feeling in the right place. I don't think I've looked for anyone's pulse since we took first aid in Girl Scouts." She looked up at me. "Dad-gum, he's dead."

"Are you sure?"

"He feels cold. I don't want to touch him anymore, just in case."

I shivered. "It's cold up here. I don't think Miss Augusta has the heat turned on. We better hurry downstairs and call somebody. Do you know him?"

"No. I can't see his face, though." She peered closer at his head. "There's something kind of familiar about him. He's got some gray in his hair, or what's left of it." Margaret Ann rocked back on her heels. "Men don't seem to mind going gray, just bald. You never hear a guy say he's having a bad hair day."

"True, but this man has had more than a bad hair day. Be careful. You don't want to disturb the crime scene."

"You read too many mysteries. Who's talking about a crime?" Margaret Ann asked. "Looks like he fell down the stairs. They're not in very good shape. I wonder what he was doing here."

"Snooping around, like we are," I said. "Maybe he broke in and was going to rob the place, although I've never seen a burglar in a camel's-hair jacket. Or wing tips."

"I've never seen a burglar at all," Margaret Ann said, standing up. "Except on *Law & Order*. Do you know they rerun that three or four times a day on TV now?"

"When did y'all get cable?"

chapter two

Ancient History, or I Used to Date the Sheriff

"Lindsey? You all right in there?" Margaret Ann's voice carried from the kitchen doorway to the backstairs bathroom.

"I'm fine," I called back. "Be out in a minute."

That was a lie. I wasn't anywhere near fine, but I knew I better get out there real quick or Mam would be barging though the door. I ran some cold water over my wrists and looked at my face in the old mirror over the sink. My natural paleness appeared positively ghostly in the dim light cast by the single bulb hanging overhead. I was also slightly green. But that was probably the mirror, its silvering so worn in places that looking in it was sort of like looking in a pool of water.

I reached in my shoulder bag for my brush and some lipstick. I best pull myself together.

Contrary to Mam's belief, my sudden departure from the

kitchen was not a delayed reaction to finding a dead man at the bottom of the attic stairs. I'd been just fine as Mam and I made our way back to the kitchen, already disassociating myself from the grim scene by imagining I was watching a movie. In my version, two pretty young women—no, make that *beautiful* young women—discovered a corpse in an old plantation house and competently took care of things. The one who looked like me (dark hair, green eyes) called 911 and reported an accident, while the one who looked like Mam (lighter hair, blue eyes) looked out the back door for two teenagers.

The reality was that Mam had taken over completely, doing all these things while I sat at the kitchen table and wondered who would play us in the movie. I wanted somebody with high cheekbones, which our family missed out on. And long legs.

Cissy and Jimmy had interrupted my casting decisions by coming in the back door, bringing a blast of cold air and dampness.

"Miss Augusta's car's not there," Cissy said breathlessly. "And the gift shop's locked. She must have gone to the historical society."

"I expect so," Mam said. "But there's been an accident upstairs. Some man we don't know. Looks like he fell. And no, don't you even think about goin' up there, Cissy, or you either, Jimmy. I've called for EMS, and I think it's best if you go on outside and wait for Jimmy's daddy while I see if I can get hold of Miss Augusta."

"But Mom, I might know him," Cissy said, even as Margaret Ann was shepherding them out the door.

"No, y'all do what I say." Mam shut the door behind them and reached for the phone on the wall.

"Jimmy's daddy?" I said. "Why would he be coming to Pinckney?"

"Because he's deputy sheriff on Indigo," Mam said. "I told you that. They moved back here from Columbia right after Labor Day."

"Wait a minute. You didn't tell me any such thing. Horace Blackwell's deputy sheriff, and no way he's Jimmy's daddy." Horace had to be sixty if he was a day, a longtime widower with a grown daughter and several grandkids over near Goose Creek.

"Of course not," Mam said. "Horace retired on account of his diabetes. I know I told you that. Will's Horace's nephew, so it just made sense for him to take the Indigo job."

"Will?" I said. "Will McLeod is deputy sheriff?" Maybe Mam didn't notice my voice rising a couple octaves, since she had the phone to her ear.

"Lindsey, I know I told you this," Mam said. "You must have forgotten. He's the chief deputy, Major McLeod." She paused. "No answer at the historical society. Maybe Miss Augusta's on her way back." She hung up the phone. "And who did you think Jimmy was? I know he doesn't favor Will much. Looks more like Darlene's family. Daddy says he's a dead ringer for Darlene's uncle when he was that age. Dead ringer. Funny how many times you use the word *dead* without thinking about it. I wonder where that expression—"

"Just a sec," I'd interrupted, and bolted for the bathroom. Let Mam think it was *dead ringer* that was turning my stomach into knots. I needed a moment to myself to process this latest information.

Will McLeod was back on Indigo. Jimmy was Will and Darlene's son. Let's see. That meant Jimmy was, what, eighteen, nineteen now? Had it really been that long?

And no way I would have forgotten Mam telling me news

like this. She thinks she's told me stuff, but then it turns out that really important news—like Aunt Cora maybe needing her knee replaced, or Will being deputy—gets lost in the stories of Cissy's cheerleading tryouts.

"Lindsey!" Mam's voice was competing now with sirens getting closer.

"I'm here," I said, opening the door and almost falling on top of her. "I'm fine. Really. Lead the way."

As if I could have stopped her. Ever since we were kids, Mam has prided herself on being the firstest with the mostest. I hung back on the porch as she directed the two EMS techs and a tall young woman in a khaki sheriff's uniform up the back stairs. The deputy, carrying a camera, had the intense beauty of a star athlete, someone like Venus Williams.

"No need to rush." Mam was talking all the while. "I'm sure he's dead, what with all that blood. Cissy heard something a couple hours ago now. Maybe you know him. I just saw the back of his head, although that looks kind of familiar. Maybe he sat in front of us at church or something."

Mam came back to the porch, where I was leaning against the rail, watching Jimmy and Cissy by his Chevy pickup. Twenty-some years ago, that would have been Will and Darlene, off in their own private world. They had been our high school's golden couple, Will the star baseball player and Key Club president, Darlene the head cheerleader and class secretary. Mam and I were lowly sophomores when they were seniors, but we'd all hung out as kids on Indigo during the summers, so even when we got to Granville County High on the mainland, joining the students from Centerville and the farm families, Will and Darlene always waved at us in the halls. That is, when they saw us. Most days, they had eyes only for each other, like Jimmy and Cissy now.

Another gold-and-white patrol cruiser came round the last curve.

"There's Will," Mam said. "He must have been further away. That deputy was Olivia Washington."

Mam, of course, hustled to Will's car, filling him in before he could even open the door. I wouldn't have to say anything any-time soon, which suited me just fine.

Will nodded in response to Mam's monologue, but then his head jerked up and he stared at the porch—at me. I smiled and tried to look calm. Right. He pulled a notebook out of his back pocket, scribbled something, and started walking toward the porch, Mam tagging along, still talking.

"I keep thinking I've seen the back of that head somewhere," she said. "But don't worry. We didn't touch him, except to try and find a pulse. Leastways, I tried to find one. Lindsey didn't touch him, did you?"

"No, I didn't," I said. "Hey, Will. Haven't seen you in a coon's age."

Coon's age. Geez, so much for impressing him with my sophistication.

"Lindsey," Will said, his narrow blue eyes looking me up and down.

He had little crinkles round his eyes now and a touch of gray in the thick, dark hair, and his jaw was heavier. But otherwise, Will McLeod, deputy sheriff, looked pretty much like Will McLeod, college senior, which was how I remembered him. Damn. The man could have developed a beer gut or a bald spot or some disfiguring skin disease—anything that didn't send me reeling back into a past I'd shut the door on long ago, or so I'd thought.

Now, all Will had to do was say my name and that door was easing its way open.

I started to say something, but Mam was there first. "We'll wait right here so you can question us further." She'd definitely been watching too many *Law & Order* reruns.

"Seems like you've told me everything already," Will said. "But I'd appreciate it if you'd stick around a few minutes, let me check things out."

Then he was gone, and I found I'd been holding my breath.

"You going to be sick again?" Mam reached out to feel my forehead.

I pulled back. "I'm fine. And no, I don't have any fever."

"You sure? You look sort of feverish. There's some kind of nasty bug going round. You probably ought not to be here in the damp. We could go back in the kitchen. Oh, wait. Here comes Miss Augusta. She's not going to know what's going on. I hope she doesn't have a spell, seeing that ambulance."

The white Cadillac, a 1984 Fleetwood, careened up the last curve, slaloming past oak trees before sliding to a stop a half-inch from the bumper of Will's cruiser.

Miss Augusta was out the car door before Mam or Cissy could get there. "Marietta? Is it Marietta, Margaret Ann? Tell me what's going on."

"No, no, it's not Marietta." Mam's voice was soothing, matter-of-fact. "Some man fell and hurt himself. EMS is here, and Will McLeod. They're taking care of things."

Miss Augusta teetered on the vintage high heels she insisted on wearing and leaned back against the car, obviously flustered. With her blue winter coat and her dyed red hair escaping in wisps from the French twist she always wore, she looked like that poster of the angry bluebird, its chest and feathers all puffed out. Taller and thinner, though.

"What man?" she said, marching toward the house. "How bad's he hurt? Where is he? I need to see him. Where's Will?" She looked up at the porch, where one of the EMS techs had just come out the door. "Young man, put out that cigarette right now. There's no smoking at Pinckney. And no, don't you dare throw that butt in the camellia bushes! Put it out in the drive and then put it in your pocket!"

Frowning, Miss Augusta turned her attention back to us. "Lindsey, I didn't see you. How are you, dear?"

I got a strong whiff of Shalimar as she gave me a brisk hug and kissed the air near my ear. I could feel the knobs of old bones beneath the coat. She stubbornly continued up the brick path, leaving Mam, myself, Cissy, and Jimmy to trail behind her, a rag-tag militia cowed by its commander. Even Mam couldn't compete with Augusta Pinckney Townsend's generalship, although she tried. Miss Augusta's late husband, Carter Townsend, had been an army colonel, but it was said that his military career had a lot to do with her behind-the-scenes management and old family connections.

"Miss Augusta, I don't really think—"

"Margaret Ann, if some stranger has hurt himself on my property, it is my duty to see that he is taken care of. Even if it does mean my insurance rates will likely go up. Cissy, where did he slip? In the front hall? I told Marietta she put too much wax on those floors last time. And with the rain we had this afternoon . . . Were his shoes wet? I bet his shoes were wet. Hardwood floors and slick soles—why, you're just asking for a sprained ankle. Didn't he see the doormat?"

"Cissy wasn't there," Mam said. She opened the front door before Miss Augusta could reach for it, then stood in front of it so we all had to stop. "Lindsey and I found him. Miss Augusta, I think we best tell you that the man appears to be seriously injured."

That was an understatement, although I had to admire Mam's handling of the situation.

Still, Miss Augusta seemed to pick up on the strain in Mam's voice. "Margaret Ann, what is it you're not saying? Dear Lord, tell me a tourist hasn't died at Pinckney Plantation."

Just then, Will appeared behind Margaret Ann. "Miss Augusta," he said. "Come on inside and sit down. I need to talk to you."

Margaret Ann stepped back so we could all enter the hallway, but Miss Augusta stood her ground.

"Tell me right now what has happened."

Will gave up. "It appears that Bradford Bentley has died from a fall."

Miss Augusta gave a gasp. "Bradford? Dead? Oh, my word." She steadied herself against the door.

"Bradford Bentley!" Mam said. "I knew I knew that head."

chapter three

Skeletons in the Attic—and Ghosts, Too

"So, what was weird about this Bentley guy's head?" J. T. asked.

"Nothing," Mam said. "Except for the part that was hurt. I just knew I'd seen that particular bald spot somewhere. And I had, at that historical-society reception they had before Christmas. I saw his face then, too, but I just didn't see it this time. I'd have known him right off if I had."

It was several hours later, and Margaret Ann was recounting the afternoon's events over leftover turkey and butterbeans, her story culminating with the identification of the dead man as the new director of the Indigo Island Historical Society.

"Miss Augusta was real upset," Mam reported. "Looked like she might be having some sort of attack at first, real pale and shaky, but one of the EMS techs checked her out, and she was all right by the time we left."

"She's not staying out there by herself?" J. T. asked.

"No, she wanted to, but Will told her there wasn't a thing she could do, and maybe she ought not to try and drive to Charleston." Mam drained her glass of tea.

"She's not coming here, is she?" J. T., one of the most laid-back men I know, looked slightly panicked. Ever since they filmed *The Patriot* in Charleston, Miss Augusta has been talking about making a television ad at Pinckney. Upon deciding that J. T. would look just the part of a Confederate officer, she'd suggested he go ahead and start growing a beard.

"No, you can still shave," Mam said, smiling at J. T.'s look of relief. "Will had me call Miss Maudie and arrange for her to stay there tonight. Olivia was going to drop her off while Will waited for the coroner and some other people. He said that even when a death is accidental, it has to be investigated. Of course, he's in charge down here. Floyd Griggs may be sheriff, but he doesn't move out of Centerville unless it's an election year. Will had Cissy fetch the guest register and told her he'd go over it with her tomorrow if he needed to."

"We didn't have that many people, except from the historical society," Cissy volunteered. "I told him I saw Mr. Bentley come in with them after lunch, but he didn't go on the tour. Neither did Aunt Cora or Miss Augusta. I didn't see him again. I thought he left with everyone else."

"Miss Augusta says he doesn't have any family, just an ex-wife somewhere," Mam said. "He was renting one of those new villas that Ray Simmons owns. I guess Will will have to check that out, too. Have you ever been inside one of them, Lindsey? I went in the model one last summer, and it was real cute, but I didn't think there was enough closet space. I guess if you were just renting for a week, it would be all right, but if it were my house, I'd want more closets."

J. T. pushed back from the table. "Honey, if you were building a storage shed, you'd want more closets."

Mam chose to ignore his gibe so as to return to the main topic. "Y'know, we could have carried Miss Augusta to Miss Maudie's. Middle House isn't that far from here. I think Will wanted us out of the way. I wonder why he didn't suggest she stay with Aunt Cora."

"Middle House is closer, and Miss Maudie has more room," I said. "Besides, whenever Miss Augusta and Aunt Cora get put out with one another, Miss Maudie mediates. She's the easygoing one of that trio."

"True," Mam agreed. "Lindsey, you've been pushing that rice around your plate for ten minutes."

"It's good," I said. "I'm just not very hungry."

"Are you sure you're not coming down with something?" She cocked her head to consider me. "You're still pale as a ghost."

"Speaking of ghosts," said Jimmy, "what was that about a ghost at Pinckney?" He was sitting on one of the barstools at Margaret Ann's counter next to Cissy, who was passing the dirty dishes to her mother.

"It's a pretty famous ghost." Mam scraped a plate into a dish for the dog. Chloe, the black-and-white cocker, stopped nosing me for a handout and headed for the kitchen.

"Didn't you ever hear about it?" I asked.

"No, ma'am, not that I remember. We didn't come down here that much when we were in Columbia, and we only moved back here when school started. I don't believe in any of that ghost stuff, anyway." He wrapped his long legs around the stool, twisting toward Cissy.

"I do," Cissy said, turning so her knees touched Jimmy's. "Remember that day I told you about having to close up by myself, 'cause Mrs. Chesnut had to leave early? I locked the door at the top of the back stairs and went and locked the front door, and when I came back, the stair door was swinging wide open. And before you say anything, I know I was there by myself. But not for long. It was too spooky. I locked that door again and came right on home."

"Who is this ghost supposed to be, anyway?" Jimmy didn't look convinced that any ghost existed.

"Oh, there are several different stories," I said. "One has it that it's the ghost of a slave girl who was forced to be the mistress of the first Pinckney. Another is that it's one of the Pinckney ancestors who wasn't right in the head." I tried to remember the word our late grandmother used to describe anyone who was mentally or physically handicapped. "He was—what did Nanny call it?—afflicted."

Mam nodded, wiping her hands on a towel and sitting at the kitchen table with me. "Supposedly, they kept him locked in a cage in the attic."

"Then there's the story that one of the Pinckney daughters fell in love with a Union soldier during the Civil War," I continued. "When her daddy found out, he locked her in the attic and told her he was going to shoot the soldier. She beat on the door, and when she couldn't get out, she broke the window to warn the soldier. But she cut her wrist on the glass so bad she bled to death before anyone could help her."

"That's the most romantic story," Cissy said. "And the saddest."

"I don't believe a word of it," Mam said. We all looked at her. "Well, if she'd cut her arm, she'd have wrapped her skirt or something around it. They were always tearing up their skirts and bandaging the wounded during the Civil War. Scarlett O'Hara wouldn't have blinked an eye about some little bitty cut, and I can't imagine one of Augusta Pinckney's ancestors being a ninny either."

"There is a cage up there," Cissy cut in. "I saw it when I helped Miss Augusta bring down the Christmas decorations. I asked her about it, but she must not have heard me, 'cause she never answered."

"Or didn't want to," I said.

"We know about the cage," Mam said. "It was there when we were your age, and no one would talk about it then. That's why I favor the crazy-ghost version, because that's the kind of thing Miss Augusta wouldn't want to talk about. That and the slave girl."

"There's other weird stuff that really does happen out at Pinckney," Cissy said. "Things get moved around and show up in different places. The other day, I was giving a tour and went to point out the old snuffbox, and when I turned around, it wasn't there."

From where I was, I could see J. T. in his recliner sleepily watching *Law & Order*. I'd had my quotient of dead bodies for one day, thank you very much. You'd have thought Mam stumbled over corpses every day, the way J. T. had taken the news. "Sounds as if Bentley was where he wasn't supposed to be," he'd said. Then he'd told Cissy he didn't want her going up the back stairs at Pinckney until he had a chance to make sure they were safe.

Margaret Ann was playing with a place mat. She can't stand not to be doing something. She was into multitasking before there was such a word. "Cissy, go slip on your costume and let me look at that hem. Jimmy, why don't you call your daddy and see if maybe he'd like to come by for pound cake and coffee? Maybe he'll know more by now."

I took another swallow of Coke. Oh, great, I thought, as Jimmy headed off to the hall phone. Just what I needed—more Will McLeod. But the last thing I wanted was for Mam to think there was any reason for my not wanting to see Will. She hadn't known then, and I didn't want her knowing now. We needed a change of subject.

"That dress of Cissy's looks like those bridesmaids' dresses we had to wear at Amy Padgett's wedding. Remember?"

"Lord, yes," said Mam. "I looked like a big old grape, and I wasn't but six months pregnant."

"Who's six months pregnant?" asked Cissy, reappearing in her Pinckney purple over her jeans.

"I was, with you, when we were in a wedding."

"That may be one of the ugliest dresses ever in my large collection of bridesmaids' dresses," I said. "And I never wore a one of them again. That's one of those great lies: 'Oh, I'm sure you'll get a lot of use out of it.' "

"How come you never got married, Aunt Lindsey?"

"Who said I didn't?"

"You got married? When? Where is he?" Cissy was looking around the room, as if a husband for me would suddenly materialize.

Margaret Ann raised an eyebrow.

"Oh, she's old enough to know," I said. "I can't believe you never let it slip before now. Dennis wasn't that bad. In fact, he was very good looking."

"He was," Mam said. "For a Yankee."

"You're married to a Yankee named Dennis?" Cissy said. "Why haven't I ever met him?"

" 'Cause it happened before you were born," I said. "The summer after my sophomore year in college, I met Dennis when I was a camp counselor in Massachusetts. We got married on the spur of the moment at the end of the summer, and it turned out to be a big mistake. I was home by Christmas and back at Chapel Hill the next semester. Then your mama and daddy got married not too long after that, and your Aunt Bonnie and I got to be co-maids of honor."

"I can't believe no one ever told me this." Cissy looked at both of us accusingly. "Do you have a picture of him?"

"You and Bonnie looked good in those red velvet dresses, admit it," Mam said.

"Except we like to burnt up. Who knew it was going to be almost eighty degrees on Indigo Island the end of January?"

I was just as glad to get away from the topic of my brief, hasty marriage, and I didn't particularly want to dig out any pictures of Dennis. Margaret Ann might notice now that Den had looked like a blonde version of Will. I'd married on the rebound, though no one knew at the time, myself included.

"Stand still and stop fidgeting," Margaret Ann ordered Cissy. "You must have been wearing flats when we measured this. We should have remembered the sneakers add a little bit of height. Good thing I left such a big hem." She got off her knees. "Go take it off and bring me my sewing box. I might as well fix it now."

"So," I said casually, waiting until Cissy was out of earshot. "How's Darlene doing these days?"

"All right, I suppose," Mam said. "I haven't seen her, although I think Jimmy went up to see her right before Christmas."

"Went where?" I said, totally confused.

"Spartanburg," Mam said. "That's where they're living."

"Who's living?"

"Darlene and that fellow she left Will for."

My jaw didn't hit the floor, but it dropped enough that Mam could tell this was the first I'd heard.

"Good grief," she said. "I could have sworn I told you all this when it happened. I know I told Bonnie. It was the talk of the island. I'm surprised your mama didn't mention it, although it may have been while they were in Florida last spring, and then right after they got back was when Daddy had that gall-bladder thing, and there was that uproar about that new development Pinck Townsend and Ray Simmons are planning. I reckon they think they can make a fortune selling deepwater lots on Crab Creek, although they want to call it Magnolia Cay or something highfalutin like that. 'Course, the county and state planning people are going to have to give 'em permits, and—"

"Margaret Ann," I interrupted. "Will? Darlene? You want to tell me what happened?"

"Well, we don't really know," she said, lowering her voice and making sure Jimmy and Cissy weren't about to rejoin us. "It seems that Darlene just up and walked out last winter, said she wanted a divorce. Turned out she'd been having an affair with this state legislator she met while she was working as a secretary for Larry Hamilton—y'know, the representative from down here. Anyway, it had been going on for quite a while, but he had his political career to think of. He was married, too, or was then. I don't know if his wife found out, or he told her, or what. I mean, it's not like you can just ask Will, although I did hear that he never suspected a thing. But I'm not sure I believe that."

She stopped. "Jimmy," she said brightly. "I'm getting ready to cut that pound cake now. You want ice cream with yours? I know J. T. will. How 'bout your daddy, is he coming over?"

"No, ma'am," Jimmy said. "He said for me to go on home and he'd see me there, but he didn't know how long he was going to be."

Mam pulled out the cake knife. "I wonder what would take so long. Guess we'll find out tomorrow. Lindsey, get that vanilla ice cream out the freezer."

I was glad to have something to do. I didn't think Jimmy had heard Mam talking about Darlene. I could hardly believe it. Well, I declare, as Aunt Cora always said. It made my head spin, the way the past kept spilling into the present. The icy air on my face felt good. Will and Darlene . . . Will and no Darlene . . .

"Lindsey, that ice cream is right in front of you, or should be."

"Sorry," I said, shutting the freezer door with some difficulty. "Have you got a whole cow in there?"

"No, just a half," Mam said. "I keep meaning to take it out to the garage freezer with the shrimp and fish, but it seems like every time I think about it, J. T. wants a steak for dinner or I get distracted."

The phone rang, as if on cue.

"Hey," said Mam. "Oh, Bonnie. You are not going to believe—"

Bonnie, having been Mam's little sister for more than thirty years, knew better than anyone how to cut her off so she could get her own two cents in, especially when calling long distance from D.C.

"You are?" Mam said. "Well, that's great. Do you need us to pick you up at the air—"

Mam nodded. "Uh-huh. Uh-huh. Well, I was going to tell you— Uh-huh. Okay, but—"

She hung up the phone. "Bonnie's flying to Charleston in the morning, some case she's working on, but Tom and the boys are still going skiing with his folks till after New Year's. She's renting a car and will be here for lunch. I tell you, she talks so fast that I didn't even have a chance to tell her about everything."

"You could call her back," I suggested. "But it's not like she knew Bradford Bentley."

"True. I guess it can wait till she gets here, and maybe we'll find out more by then. I want to call Beth Chesnut and see what she knows about Bradford. Aunt Cora, too, if her line ever stops being busy. And I still need to hem Cissy's costume. Let's just hope Bonnie packs something black."

"Why?"

"Really, Lindsey," Mam said. "We've got a funeral to go to."

I hardly noticed the drive home. I was dead tired—that word again. But I was also keyed up. As I opened a can of Science Diet for Peaches, who was winding around my ankles and purring up a storm in anticipation, I wondered who I could call and talk to.

That reminded me to check the answering machine, something I did automatically when I walked in the door at my duplex in Charlotte but never thought about here. Mama had probably called to let me know they had arrived, but I knew that if there had been any other news, she or Aunt Boodie would have called Mam.

I put Peaches' dish next to his water bowl on the blue plastic place mat on the floor by the counter.

"Here you go, big guy," I said, stroking his back as he attacked the food like he hadn't eaten in six months, instead of six hours. "Did we get any calls? Or did you make any while I was gone? Betcha you tried on some of my clothes, though."

That was my theory as to why he spent so much time in my closets at home and here, although orange hairs in the laundry basket at the back indicated his favorite napping place.

The answering machine was flashing.

"Hello, Lindsey, this is your mother."

Like I wouldn't know her voice. Mama always sounded uncomfortably formal when she had to leave a message. Daddy said he never understood why she or Boodie had to use a phone anyway, they talked so loud. And it was true that their voices did carry. I could lose Mama in the grocery store and just stand still and listen, and soon I'd hear her over in produce or by the frozen foods.

"I thought you would be at home," Mama's voice continued. "Maybe you are at Margaret Ann's. I wanted to let you know we're at the port and getting ready to board. Boodie thought she'd left her tote bag at home, but it was in the backseat. See you next Saturday. Be sweet. We love you. Good-bye, now."

I could hear her carefully replacing the receiver, as if it might break. I looked at the mantel clock. It was after ten. They were on the high seas by now.

Peaches had scarfed his dinner and was now staring at the empty dish as if seconds would magically appear. "Dream on," I said.

I wished I could call Vaughn, my college roommate and still my closest confidante, but I knew she was at her in-laws' in Raleigh. She was the only person, other than myself and Will, who knew what had happened—and hadn't happened—back then. She would be very interested to hear that he was back in the picture—the scene of the crime, so to speak.

Guilt washed over me. A man had died today, and here I was thinking about blue eyes and long-ago kisses.

"Peaches, I'm going to bed and read," I said, scooping him up over my shoulder. "Lord, you weigh a ton. Has Daddy been sneaking you turkey?"

I'd been saving the new Ian Rankin until after Christmas, but I wasn't in the mood for a mystery, even if it did take place in faraway Edinburgh. Good thing I'd read Carolyn Hart's *Sugarplum Dead* last year. That really would have been too close to home.

I looked at the stack of old paperbacks in the little bookcase that had doubled as a nightstand in my room since I was a kid. *Anne of Green Gables*. There was a thought. No, wait. Jane Austen. Perfect. *Pride and Prejudice* or *Persuasion*. Elizabeth Bennet was my favorite heroine, but I was about to be persuaded by *Persuasion* and its story of an old love returning. Then the phone rang. Peaches looked up from his bath at the foot of the bed as I picked up the portable I'd brought upstairs.

"Hello."

"Lindsey?"

"Hey, Will," I said.

chapter four

Who's Bringing Congealed Salad?

"Do y'all think this green dress will be okay?" Bonnie asked. "It's either this or the red trouser suit. I mean, shoot, it's the holidays. I wasn't planning on a funeral."

It was early the next afternoon, and Bonnie had rolled up in her white rental Toyota a half-hour earlier. Mam had finally got to fill her in on the events at Pinckney. Bonnie was suitably impressed by our quick-thinking actions—Mam's, anyway.

"How green is it?" asked Mam, stirring lime Jell-O at her porcelain cook-top.

"It's definitely green," I said as Bonnie unveiled the dress from her monogrammed garment bag. "Pretty, though. That thin wool doesn't scratch, either."

"It's the color of my congealed salad," Mam said.

"Only if you add cream cheese," defended Bonnie. "Besides, I have this great designer scarf I found at a little consignment store in Alexandria."

"Does it have any black in it?" I asked.

Finding something black to wear to the funeral wasn't going to be a problem for me. My closet was a black hole, in more ways than one. A journalist could never have too much black, I had long ago decided. You could dress it up or dress it down; you could blend into a crowd. And it made packing easy, although I always had to remember to pack a clothes brush too, ever since the first time I covered a cat show and came home with enough hair on my black jeans to qualify as an entry in the Persian category.

"Well, you definitely can't wear pants, even if they weren't red," Mam said. "I don't have anything dark that would be long enough, and neither does Lindsey."

Bonnie's taller and smaller than us. And a whole lot blonder. We could hate her for this, but she's too nice and normal. Besides which, she is also endearingly uncoordinated. She'd already told us that she didn't much mind missing the ski trip with Tom's athletically inclined family. "It's embarrassing," she'd said. "I'm still on the bunny slope, and the boys are like Junior Olympians."

While waiting for Bonnie, Mam and I had spent the morning separately trying to find out more about Bradford Bentley.

Will hadn't told me much about Bentley's death when he'd called, just that he wanted to talk to me sometime today.

"I think I told you everything already," I'd said. "And I'm sure Mam did."

"I want to go over a few details again. And I'd like to see you. It's been a long time."

"Yes, it has." I'd forced myself not to ask whose fault that was.

There was silence on the other end, then, "I'll let you get some sleep. We can talk tomorrow."

"Will," I'd said quickly before he could hang up. "Is there something you're not saying about this afternoon? He—Bradford Bentley—fell down the stairs and hit his head, right? There's nothing suspicious, is there?"

"Good night, Lindsey. See you tomorrow."

The Charleston paper hadn't been any more forthcoming this morning, offering only an inside item in the regional news roundup. A man had died in an apparent fall at a house on Pinckney Plantation Drive on Indigo Island. The Granville County Sheriff's Department was investigating. The victim's name had not been released, pending notification of next of kin.

Duh. There was only one house on Pinckney Plantation Drive, and that was Pinckney Plantation. Miss Augusta would be pleased, though, that the story didn't say the director of the Indigo Island Historical Society had met his death on her attic stairs.

Mam had agreed when I talked to her on the phone.

"He's in the obituaries, though. Turn to the last page of the local section, and he's listed under Granville County, and then there's a short funeral notice about halfway down the page. Doesn't say much we didn't already know. He was fifty-two, originally from Richmond, had degrees from William and Mary and UVA and taught at the College of Charleston. The memorial service is at ten tomorrow at Indigo Island Chapel. Guess they didn't want to wait till Monday. I thought maybe Stuhr's in Charleston would handle the arrangements, but Otis is doing him."

"Otis Heywood's is the only funeral home in Centerville," I

pointed out. "Besides, it's only thirty minutes away, instead of more than an hour. I see that, in lieu of flowers, we're supposed to send donations to the historical society."

"I hate these paid obituaries," Mam complained. "It doesn't say anything about how he died. Just this 'entered into eternal rest.' I know it's up to the families to put in whatever they want, and I tell you, some of them read like a book, listing all the relatives. But I always want to know how come they're dead, especially if it's a youngish person—like whether they were killed in a car wreck, or if it was cancer or a heart attack."

"Or a fall down the stairs. That much we know."

Mam and I had just started comparing notes at her house when Bonnie honked from the oyster-shell drive.

"So," Bonnie said, now that the funeral-attire decision had been made by default, "did this Bradford guy fall, or was he pushed?"

Mam and I looked at each other. We had been wondering that ourselves, but even Mam hadn't yet dared voice the thought. It was just too outlandish to think we could have discovered a murder victim. Indigo wasn't immune to crime, especially during the spring and summer, when rowdy teens drank too much and drove too fast and fights broke out on beach-house porches. The occasional domestic dispute erupted on the north side of the island, usually involving Futches and Smoaks, Indigo's version of the Hatfields and the McCoys, until they started marrying each other. There also were break-ins, especially during the winter, when fewer people were living on the island. And the DEA patrolled the coastal rivers with an eye out for drug runners. But murder?

"Well, he wasn't what you'd call popular," I said.

Mam snorted. "That's an understatement. Hardly anybody liked him, except a couple of old maids and desperate divorcées—and I don't mean like you, Lindsey, before you climb up on that high-horse career-woman thing. Lura Maitland was always taking him casseroles, although if he ever ate one of her shrimp-with-black-olive messes, he'd have run in the opposite direction. Miss Augusta was his real champion. She's the one who insisted last October that he be named executive director of the historical society."

"But where was he from?" Bonnie said. "Was he related?"

"Well, not to us," I said. "And not to anyone on the island that we know of, or at least that's what was in the paper and what Beth Chesnut told Mam this morning. You know Beth—she's head of the volunteers at Pinckney and runs the gift shop. She said he was from Richmond originally but had been teaching at the college in Charleston the last couple of years. He was doing some research for a paper on Indigo when the society opening came up."

"But that doesn't pay much," Bonnie said.

"I know," Mam said. "That's why Miss Maudie's grandson took the job teaching in Columbia. He'd been doing it, and most members wanted someone else local, like Beth, who could have used any money, what with three kids. But Miss Augusta was insistent, because Bradford had all these academic credentials and connections. Plus, he already had some grant money from the state, so he could afford to take it. I think she thought that in the long run, it would help Pinckney, too. And what Miss Augusta says goes, when it comes to the historical society."

"And Aunt Cora doesn't like that one bit," I said. "Those two have been playing tug of war for years as to who knows more island history, although Miss Maudie's probably forgotten more than the two of them put together. And Aunt Cora didn't like Bradford either. She didn't come right out and say so this morning when I talked to her on the phone. Just said, 'Poor man, it's a real shame, and there's no need to go speaking ill of the dead.' Then she started fuming about how Augusta Pinckney Townsend thought she was Miss Almighty, taking over the funeral arrangements before Bradford was barely cold."

He had looked cold enough yesterday when we found him.

"I don't know who else would have planned the funeral," Mam said. "There's that ex-wife somewhere, but Miss Augusta's the one who knew him best down here, and I'm sure she talked to his lawyer in Charleston before she went ahead. You know, people who die during the holidays really have it rough, 'cause lots of folks are out of town or have plans. Not that it makes any difference to the dead person, I suppose. But if it were me, I'd want all my friends there."

"Bradford was kind of short on friends," I reminded her. "Evidently, he rubbed a lot of folks the wrong way."

"Do tell," said Bonnie, leaning her elbows on the kitchen table.

"He made Sally Simmons cry, 'cause he told her she just married her way on the island, and everyone knew she was just a mill girl from Lyman," Mam said. "And he told Elizabeth Smith he wouldn't hang her art students' work at the museum anymore, and then he told Mr. Bennie to take down his display of Indian arrowheads because they looked like fake ones. The worst of it may have been when he said he was taking Mount Zion off the tour this coming year because it wasn't the original building."

"But that's the oldest black church in the Low Country," Bonnie said.

"I know," Mam said. "I told you it was bad. Hand me that glass dish, please."

Bonnie complied, casting a suspicious eye at the lime Jell-O.

Mam caught her glance. "I used all the red one at Christmas, and I haven't been to Piggly Wiggly yet," she said. "I hope they have some of the sparkling white grape. Oh, and Bradford hired a caterer from Charleston for the society's Christmas party at Pinckney, instead of the Episcopal church ladies. That's when Martha Bridwell washed her hands of him and the society."

"They still don't sound like reasons to push someone down the stairs," Bonnie said.

"We don't know if he was pushed or not," I said. "It could have been an accident. Mam just doesn't have enough drama in her life."

"Oh, do," Mam said, a hint of exasperation in her voice. "You wouldn't mind some excitement either. And you can spend some time with Will. And don't cut your eyes at me like that, Lindsey Lee Fox. You're the one that said you were fancy-free at the moment. Will McLeod is the most eligible man on Indigo, now that Bradford Bentley's gone and gotten himself killed."

"What, you mean Elwood Small isn't still available?" Bonnie asked with a sly grin. Elwood was a confirmed bachelor and drunk who smelled strongly of fish, which was no wonder, considering he rented a room above Tradd Seafood and crewed on the shrimp boats whenever he ran out of money and booze.

"No, no woman has yet snapped up Elwood," Mam said dryly. "And I forgot we have another single man. Luis Rivera. He's one of Miller Caldwell's new farm managers. Kinda quiet and keeps to himself, but definitely easy on the eyes. Still, I think Will's the better catch."

"For heaven's sake," I said. "I haven't seen Will in twenty years, and I'm not in what you'd call a fishing mood." Time to change the subject, and I knew just how to do it. "How is Kit Caldwell?"

"That woman!" Mam was off and running. "She thinks she can move down here from up north and take over, just because her husband's rich, although I still don't understand where that money came from. I thought he was in real estate, but she told me at the Turtle Watch fund-raiser that they wouldn't be here except for fizzbos and flipping. I had no idea what she was talking about, but I wasn't going to give her the satisfaction, so I nodded my head and asked her if she'd been to New York recently. She flies up there for weekends to go shopping and 'take in a show or two,' as she puts it. There's not any Broadway show call 'Fizzbo,' is there?"

I shook my head. "For Sale by Owner," I translated. "Fizzbo."

Bonnie nodded. "And flipping is when people buy houses, patch them up with some paint, and resell them right away at a profit. Depending on the market and interest rates, you can make a lot of money. Or you can lose your shirt if you put too much into fixing up a place and then it sits there for months and doesn't sell. Sounds like the Caldwells did all right, though."

"I'll say." Mam swished water in the Revereware pot she'd used for the Jell-O. "That probably explains how come they bought Hillcrest and are going to restore it."

"Hillcrest?" I said. "How are they going to restore something that's not there anymore? It's just land and some bricks from the foundation."

"I don't know, but Kit declared she and Miller were going to, and I quote, 'restore Hillcrest to its former glory.' "

Her imitation of Kit's Yankee twang was right on the money. The Caldwells were relative newcomers to Indigo, having ventured off the Intracoastal Waterway one day to tie their yacht at the marina overnight. Instead of continuing to south Florida, where Miller had some property, they'd instead bought Harry Chisholm's old farm and tomato-packing house. To give them credit, they'd made it a profitable concern again, judging by the acres they planted every summer and the number of red trucks lined up at the drawbridge at harvest time. But they hadn't exactly endeared themselves to the islanders, using migrant laborers, mostly Mexicans and some Haitians, instead of local workers. And although Miller was known as a nice fellow who played a good game of golf, Kit's ash-blonde haughtiness and aspirations to social grandeur set a lot of people's teeth on edge, including Margaret Ann's.

"I'm guessing Miss Augusta doesn't think much of this Hillcrest plan, if it's going to take away from Pinckney," Bonnie said. "It was built around the same time, or even before Pinckney. But didn't it burn down eons ago? How do they even know what it looked like?"

"Evidently, there are a couple of drawings and paintings, and there are detailed descriptions in a Chisholm family diary about the interior and the furnishings," Mam said. "I think Miller was consulting with Bradford about whether he might know something, too. Naturally, Kit's been volunteering for every historical-society committee in sight. I'm sure she was probably at Pinckney yesterday with those state people."

"I don't suppose we could put her on our list of suspects just because you don't like her," Bonnie said. "Maybe irritating Kit was having a secret affair with obnoxious Bradford, and they'd been meeting in the attic at Pinckney."

"Yes," I said. "And in the throes of passion, he accidentally rolled down the steps. Dying in his wing tips for the love of Kit Caldwell."

"Oh, you two," Mam said. "Y'all are such smarty-britches when you get together."

Bonnie and I grinned.

"The defense rests," she said. "What's for lunch? They don't even give you peanuts on the plane anymore, just some pretzel mix. I'm starving."

Bonnie has been an apparently effortless size six for years, even since Ben and Sam, now six and four, were born. Mam and I had warned her that she was going to have to start watching her weight when she hit thirty, but it hadn't happened. That was more than five years ago, and she was still eating what she wanted.

Mam, who keeps trim with a treadmill and Slim-Fast, raised her eyebrows.

"The boys run it off me," Bonnie said. "Can you believe Tom wanted to give them drum sets for Christmas? I told him he better make me a reservation at the hollerin' house then. Did you know he'd never heard of that? Thought I was talking about some hotel."

"We are always being threatened with the hollerin' house when we were little," I said, referring to the nearby branch of the state mental hospital. "I can remember Aunt Cora saying either we were going or she was, if we didn't stop making such a racket, although it was Jack who made all the noise." My younger brother was born not quite three months after Bonnie, our mothers having failed to exactly coordinate their pregnancies the second time around.

"I got a Christmas card from him and Jill," Bonnie said, opening the refrigerator door.

Mam leaned over her shoulder. "You want turkey or tuna fish salad?"

"Tuna. I'm getting pretty tired of turkey. I want brown bread, though, not that white air stuff." She unscrewed the lid off the jar of Duke's. "I know you already have Miracle Whip in it, but I like real mayonnaise. Is this tea sweet?"

Mam nodded. We exchanged looks of amazement and envy as Bonnie slathered two thick slices of bread.

"Hope our mamas are having a good time. Maybe shipboard bridge and bingo will make up for missing all this excitement," Bonnie said between bites. "They're both like Nanny. They do love funerals."

"We can sign their names in the register," Mam said. "We used to do that for Nanny all the time, when she felt like she ought to go pay her respects but didn't really care for the deceased."

"Heck," I said. "Then let's sign her name, too."

chapter five

Holidays Make for Small Funerals

"That green wool looks great on you, Bonnie," I said. "And I'm sorry that Christmas is over, or you could just wrap up that scarf and give it to me."

"Thanks," Bonnie said, getting out of one side of Mam's backseat while Cissy slid out the other. "I don't know why I was so worried about what to wear. It just doesn't seem to matter as much anymore, no matter where you go. There are always going to be people more dressed up than you"—she nodded at Miss Maudie Frampton, dressed in black crepe and a hat and using her silver-headed cane to slowly make her way across the oak-leaf-strewn grass—"and people who don't look nearly as good"—she frowned in the direction of Cap Lockhart from the filling station.

"I told you he wouldn't wear a tie," J. T. grumbled, tugging on his. "Suzanne couldn't get him into one for their wedding, and I bet he won't be buried in one either."

"They're not burying Bradford," Margaret Ann said, looking proper in a navy suit. "Beth told me last night he's being cremated and his ashes sent to Richmond. This is just a memorial service."

"Same difference," J. T. said. "There's just not a casket for people to stare at."

"I know it sounds morbid," Mam said, "but I like an open casket. It's your last chance to see somebody."

"Some body is right," Bonnie pointed out. "Most times, it's a body that doesn't even look like the person."

I didn't want to get into a discussion of corpses. "I've been inside already," I said. "There's a picture on the altar."

I'd arrived at the old plantation chapel early and spent some time admiring its quiet dignity. Long ago, it had been the only church on Indigo. The adjoining graveyard was studded with mossy, tilted headstones proclaiming the history and heritage of Indigo back to before the American Revolution, even.

"Picture of what?" Margaret Ann asked.

"Of Bradford Bentley, silly," I said. "The deceased. You know, the reason we are all here. At least I assume it's him, seeing as how I never saw his face. But I don't believe I've ever seen a studio portrait of Jesus in horn-rims."

"Don't be blasphemous, Lindsey," Mam admonished as we filed up the chapel's worn wooden steps. "It's still a church, even if it's hardly ever used as one. Is Aunt Cora here yet?"

"Up there on the left," I said. "I figure she's sitting pretty much on top of where Great-Great-Uncle Trout is buried."

"Really, Lindsey!" Mam's loud whisper caused several people to turn their heads toward us. No one in our family really knows how to whisper. If anything, Mam's whisper carries farther than her regular voice.

Bonnie pursed her lips, trying not to laugh. I slipped past both of them so I could sit next to Aunt Cora, who reached out to hold my hand as I kissed her papery cheek. Her left arm was in a sling.

"What happened?" I asked quietly. "Are you all right?"

"It's nothing, dear," she said. "I went to get something off the top shelf of the closet last night and strained my shoulder. That's the one with bursitis. This sling just takes some of the weight off."

"Do you need to see the doctor?"

"Oh, no, I just take me some Bufferin," she said.

Aunt Cora stiffened, and I looked to see Miss Augusta walking toward the front of the church, steadied by the arm of her nephew Pinck Townsend. He had lost some hair and gained a few pounds since I'd last seen him but otherwise looked the very image of middle-aged prosperity. His wife, Belinda, a brittle blonde, walked behind, her gaze indicating her mind was as far as possible from Indigo. She was probably wishing she was at the Talbots after-Christmas sale. Or at the country club. Other than shopping, Belinda was heavily into the ABCs—alcohol, bridge, and cigarettes.

The short pews were filling quickly. Some at the service were obviously people the dead man had known from Charleston, maybe colleagues from the college. A handsome black man with salt-and-pepper hair sat next to a petite woman whose Italian leather shoes and handbag probably cost more than I made in a year. Her heavy gold bracelets clinked as she pulled at her black skirt in a vain effort to cover her knees. I wondered who she was. I recognized many of the other faces, including Mam's friend, the gossipy Beth, with her husband, Harold, and their oldest girl. What was her name? Mary Beth? Beth Ann? I was just about to ask Bonnie if she knew when Mam leaned in to whisper at both of us.

"Pink roses," she said.

"So?" Bonnie said. The large arrangement almost overshadowed the picture of Bradford Bentley. "Better than poinsettias, or carnations."

"Or glads," Mam said. "Remember those awful orange ones that Irene put on her husband's casket? 'Course, she was going to divorce him after the Gator Bowl, but he had that heart attack first. No, I was just wondering who paid for the roses. They must have cost a fortune this time of year."

Mam, who could out-Martha Martha Stewart in most departments, had recently become obsessed with flowers. After years of occasionally helping friends with floral arrangements for weddings and parties, she was starting a small business. She already had three weddings lined up for spring, and a fiftieth-wedding-anniversary celebration. But she was still trying to come up with the right name for her enterprise, having discarded Blossoms and Bows as too cutesy and Flowers by Design as too formal. J. T.'s suggestion of Petal Pushers had been rejected outright.

Now, I could hear her muttering under her breath: "In the Pink. Rose in Bloom."

"Shush," Bonnie said. "They're starting."

As Charles Hendricks, the young rector from the Episcopal church, began his prayer, I closed my eyes, but not before noticing how white Aunt Cora's knuckles were as she clasped her pocketbook. I wondered what was bothering her. Maybe her shoulder hurt more than she said.

"Amen," we all said in unison.

The service was from the *Book of Common Prayer*, as far as I could tell. Our family is mostly Baptist and Methodist. Mama and Aunt Boodie grew up Baptist, but when Mama married Daddy, she joined the Foxes at the Methodist church. I always told people I was the product of a mixed marriage, 'cause I'd ended up going to Indigo Baptist with Mam and Nanny and Aunt Cora almost as much as to Fishing Creek Methodist. Mam, Bonnie, and I had double doses of Bible school in the summer, and in high school, Mam came with me to Methodist Youth Fellowship 'cause she had a thing for Chris Jenkins. That was fine with me. Will McLeod was Methodist, too, and I spent many a Sunday morning watching the back of his head in the pew right in front of us. It was about the only time he wasn't with Darlene. She was Presbyterian.

I hadn't seen Will when we came in, but I was sure he was there. Probably behind us with Jimmy, which would explain why Cissy kept flipping her hair over her shoulder. I started to smile but caught myself. This was a funeral, after all.

"In the short time he was with us on Indigo, Bradford Bentley made his mark on this community," the Reverend Hendricks said.

A diplomatic way to put it, I thought.

"I'd now like to call on someone who knew Bradford both as a friend and a colleague, the distinguished historian Dr. Henry Colleton."

The handsome man I'd noticed earlier walked to the front of the chapel, then surveyed the congregation with a serious look.

"First, I'd like to extend my condolences to Bradford's dearest friend and supporter on this island, Mrs. Townsend"—he nodded at Miss Augusta, who inclined her head in acknowledgment—"as well as to someone many of you might not know, Penelope Upchurch"—he nodded to the woman he'd been sitting next to.

When we all turned to look, her head nod seemed more like a duck-and-cover move. Mam craned over J. T.'s shoulder for a better look, but Miss Maudie's hat was in her way.

"Although Miss Upchurch and Bradford divorced some years ago, they remained friends and had the greatest admiration for each other's work in their respective fields, Low Country plantation history on Bradford's part, as I'm sure you know—and which is how I came to know him, through my own work with slave narratives—and Penelope's study of colonial art and antiques."

I wasn't sure how many people heard that last bit, as they were still taking in that the dead man's ex-wife was in the church. I'd seen Miss Augusta's head swivel at the news.

Henry Colleton continued, apparently unaware that his audience's attention was divided now. Was he about to drop another bombshell?

No. Colleton's remarks turned out to be what you'd expect, mostly about Bradford's fine reputation as a scholar. Like the Reverend Hendricks, he skirted the abrasive-personality issue, calling Bradford "strong minded, and a man of conviction," but he seemed sincere when he said he would miss him.

After another prayer, we all spilled out into the pale winter sunshine. Mam made a beeline for Penelope Upchurch, but she wasn't fast enough. Bradford's ex-wife—did you become a widow if your ex died?—hurriedly backed a black BMW off the grass and was halfway to the highway by the time J. T. ushered Aunt Cora to her Olds. I noticed how everyone gave Aunt Cora and her land yacht a wide berth. It had been a tossup last year if she'd pass the eye exam for her driver's license.

"No, she didn't bribe anybody either," said Will, standing suddenly at my elbow and reading my mind. "We all kind of keep an eye out for her, and Miss Augusta, too."

Will grinned, and I smiled back. For the moment, we were comfortable with each other and the quiet. He had called again yesterday while I was at Mam's, saying he'd be tied up most of the day but still wanted to get together, probably sometime after the funeral.

"Here y'all are," said Mam. "We gotta run carry Bonnie back to the house so she can get some lunch and get to Charleston for that meeting she flew down here for. But I wanted to tell you—and Will, you should know this, too—Cissy says that Penelope person was at Pinckney that day with the historical-society people. And so was Henry Colleton."

"Thanks, Margaret Ann," Will said. "Let me go catch him before he leaves."

The professor was talking to the Reverend Hendricks. Mam and J. T. headed over to where Bonnie was paying her respects to Miss Augusta. I started to follow but then saw Marietta standing off by one of the pecan trees.

"That is some hat," I said, admiring the wide-brimmed, feathered concoction. "You look real regal. I'm not sure I can get under it to give you a kiss."

"I wondered when you were going to come see me, child," Marietta said, holding my hands in hers.

"You'd already gone when I was at Pinckney the other day."

"Don't I know it! A good thing, too, although I'm real sorry you and Margaret Ann had to see such a sight. Like I told Mr.

Will, I haven't been up those stairs in months, my knees get so bad in the winter. Don't know what I'd a done if I'd been there and heard something. But I didn't hear anything 'cept them historic folk listening to Cissy. She remind me of when you and her mama used to give those tours. She sure growing up fast."

"I know," I said. "But you look just the same as when I was Cissy's age. You don't change a bit—only your hats."

"Oh, go on now," she said, preening. "Don't you be trying to fool this old woman. I got myself a mirror, and I reckon I know how I look. That's why I like this hat. Hides my face."

"Do," I said. "You like that hat because it has so many feathers."

"That's the truth, child, indeed it is," she said, chuckling. Then her face turned serious as she looked across the churchyard to where Miss Augusta was holding court. "I'm worried about Miss Augusta, though. She don't look so good. She's taking this real hard."

"Did you know Mr. Bentley well?" I asked.

"Him!" Marietta sniffed. "He was too uppity to have anything to do with the likes of me. You know, like that Miz Caldwell. Looks at you every time like she never seen you before. He wasn't that bad, but almost. But he treated Miss Augusta real nice. Listened to all her stories, took her to ride in that fancy black car of his."

"I wonder what he was doing in the attic."

"Oh, he acted like he own Pinckney. Went pretty much anywhere he wanted. I told Mr. Will that. 'Bout all I could tell him." Her attention was caught by a blue Buick pulling up. "There's my sister's girl Louelma. She's going to carry me over to Ravenel to see her mama and our cousins from Atlanta this afternoon. They have to leave to go back tomorrow."

"You have a nice time," I said, opening the car door for her and nodding to the plump lady behind the wheel. "Mind you don't crush any of those pretty feathers. It was good to see you."

"I'll see you and Margaret Ann next week." Marietta was negotiating the shoulder belt so it didn't catch the brim of her hat. "She said y'all are going to help take down the decorations at Pinckney."

That was the first I'd heard of it, but I smiled and waved Marietta off. It was typical of Mam to volunteer us without telling me. She was still talking to Miss Augusta, while Bonnie stood by impatiently. Bonnie saw me and pointed at her watch. I'd create a diversion so she could get Mam home and herself on the way to Charleston. But before I could say anything, Miss Augusta did.

"Oh, look. There's Jamie now. The dear boy didn't have to come, but he said he'd be here."

That the dear boy was late didn't seem to bother her. We watched as the occupant of a dark green Lexus SUV made his unhurried way toward us, while Miss Augusta headed to meet him halfway. This must be Pinck and Belinda's son. I hadn't seen him since he was a little boy and Mam and I had been roped into baby-sitting for him at Pinckney one afternoon so he wouldn't disrupt the tour groups. He'd been a sandy-haired hellion then but now was unmistakably a preppie in standard-issue khakis, Oxford shirt, and navy blazer.

"Mm," Mam said, voicing my own thoughts. "At least he's wearing socks with his Topsiders."

Topsiders. They were ubiquitous, I thought, rummaging through the closet in my old room that night in search of a flannel shirt. So far, I'd found a couple of Daddy's extra golf irons, Jack's high-school letter jacket, and a worn-out, salt-stained pair of Topsiders that were probably older than Jamie Townsend.

Too bad he wasn't ten years older, or I was ten years younger. I'd never been especially attracted to frat rats—too uptight, too much money and privilege—but there was a hint of the hellion I remembered in Jamie's brown eyes and easygoing smile. Mam had said he'd just got his master's in urban planning. That was when she'd called me this afternoon, interrupting my post-lunch nap.

"Coming Up Roses," she said.

"What?"

"Coming Up Roses. That's what I'm going to call my business. I was thinking of those pink roses at the service, and it just came to me."

"I like it," I said. "Lots better than Perfect Posies."

" 'Coming Up Roses. Flowers for weddings and special events,' " she said proudly. "That's what I'm going to put on my business cards and on my web site."

"I didn't know you had a web site."

"I don't yet, but there's a guy J. T. works with that does web design on the side, and he says he'll be my web master if I'll do his daughter's wedding for just the cost of the flowers."

"Sounds like a good deal," I said.

"Yes, even though web masters remind me of giant spiders. And I hate spiders almost as much as you do, even though I try to remember your advice and think of *Charlotte's Web*. Anyway, I was on the computer and was going to do an Internet search on Bradford, only there's something wrong with the modem. Why don't you see what you can find on your laptop?"

When I checked later, I didn't find anything on Bradford that we didn't already know, but I did on Penelope Upchurch. If this was the same person, and it sounded like it, she lived in Philadelphia now and was co-owner of an antiques shop.

I'd checked my e-mail while I was at it. Mostly spam, although my boss, Andrew, editor-owner of *Perfect Pet*, sent New Year's greetings and suggested we touch base next week about story ideas. By the time I'd replied, there had just been time for a sunset walk on the beach. Peaches and I had shared a turkey sandwich for dinner, then fallen asleep watching the old movie *Laura* on TV. Good thing I already knew how it ended.

Wide awake now and chilly, I had just found a lumberjack plaid flannel shirt in the closet when the front doorbell rang downstairs, competing with the James Taylor I'd put on the CD player. Good grief, it was after eleven. Who on earth?

"Cissy, Jimmy," I said, unlatching the door and letting them in. They smelled of the outdoors—wood smoke and salt and cold all mixed together.

"We need your advice," Cissy said, leaning down to unlace her damp boots. There were leaves in her hair.

Jimmy saw them, too, and his face flushed. "It's not what you're thinking."

"Lindsey's cool," Cissy said. "She's not going to tell Mama."

"Tell your mama what?" I said, walking over to turn down "Country Road" so she couldn't see my face. Surely, history wasn't about to repeat itself. Cissy was just sixteen, and I know kids grow up faster these days, but they also grow up smarter.

"That we went out to Pinckney tonight," Cissy said. "Daddy'd have a fit if he knew, especially since Mr. Bentley died. He's even talking about me quitting work, and I can't do that because I'm saving the money for that church trip to Mexico next summer.

Besides, Miss Augusta counts on me to—"

"So why do you need my advice?" The girl could rattle on just like her mother.

"Because of this." Jimmy pulled a large bone from inside his coat. It was the length of my arm but old, yellow, and crumbling.

"It's a bone," Cissy said.

"I can see that."

"But what kind?" Jimmy asked. "It's too big to be a dog, and I don't think it's a deer, 'cause I've seen lots of those, and they just don't look like this."

"Where did you find it? I mean, where at Pinckney? Jimmy, put it over there on top of those newspapers for recycling and come sit down and tell me what happened." I made a grab for Peaches, who was sniffing at the bone, back arched and fur standing on end. He bounded from the hallway toward the stairs and my bedroom.

"Well, we were over on the other side of the road from Pinckney, in those woods going down to the river," Cissy said. "Jimmy wanted to show me where he wants to put a deer stand, if Miss Augusta will let him."

Yeah, right, I thought. Then again, the truck would have been a lot warmer, and Cissy had told me Jimmy loved hunting.

"It's kind of far back in there," Jimmy said. "I had the flashlight, though, and I knew where we were. Anyway, Cissy thought she heard a deer, but I knew she didn't, 'cause a buck would have smelled us coming a mile away with that flowery stuff she wears. Y'know, you really shouldn't shower for at least a day before huntin'."

"Eeew, gross," said Cissy, poking Jimmy's arm. "I'm not going hunting with you if I can't wash my hair."

"I haven't asked you to yet." He grabbed her hand. "And who says I'm going to?"

"Okay, okay," I cut in. "The bone?"

"Jimmy was raking up some leaves and moving some branches around, and then I saw it sticking up out of the ground, and so we dug it up."

And brought it to good old Aunt Lindsey, whose experience with bones, other than steaks on the grill, was decidedly limited.

The doorbell sounded again. Honestly, who now? Had I invited the entire island to drop by?

"I saw Jimmy's truck as I was driving home—"

"—and you thought you'd see why your son was here." I finished Will's sentence for him.

He saw the bone right off. "What's this?" He picked it up and turned it over. "Where did you get it?"

"We found it, Dad. That's the reason we came here, to ask what to do with it. Cissy knew Lindsey was up, and I knew you were on the late shift tonight and didn't want to bother you."

"Jimmy was showing Cissy where he wants to put a deer stand out near Pinckney," I told Will, who seemed to think that this was a reasonable explanation for two teens tromping around the woods at night.

"I'll take charge of this," he said, looking more closely at the bone, his brow furrowed. "Jimmy, you can show me tomorrow where you found this. I think you best get Cissy home before her mother starts calling the sheriff."

"That's you," Cissy said. "Oh, I get it." She laughed. "That's pretty funny."

"And no, I won't say anything to your mother," I said, closing the door on them. "Not yet."

Will had obviously decided he was going to stay awhile, because he'd shed his jacket and was standing in front of the fire. The man had a knack for catching me in my glamour mode—sweat pants and Jack's flannel shirt over a faded University of North Carolina T-shirt.

"Nice outfit," he said.

Was I so transparent?

"So what about this bone?" I said, settling on the sofa and hugging my knees to my chest. At least I had on a bra. "Is it what I think it is?"

"Depends on what you think it is."

"Jimmy says it's not a deer, although I wouldn't know. And he's right that it looks too big to be a dog. And Indigo isn't home to any lions or tigers or bears—oh, my. So my guess is that it's human."

chapter six

Please Don't Pass the Whitman's

"So, is it human?" Mam asked the next morning after church. "What does Will think?"

"He didn't really say," I told her, looking down at my second Coke of the morning. I'd almost nodded off a couple of times during the substitute preacher's sermon on the wise men, and hadn't really woken up till the end, when the small congregation had stood to sing "We Three Kings." Afterwards, I'd driven straight to Margaret Ann's and let myself in with the key she keeps under an empty terra-cotta pot near the back steps. The Methodists always get out earlier than the Baptists.

I stifled another yawn. I had given her and Bonnie a highly edited version of the previous night's events, saying only that Jimmy had found the bone out near Pinckney, and that Cissy suggested showing it to me on impulse as they were driving home, and that I had then shown it to Will. No need for them to know that Cissy had been in on the discovery. Nor did I need to tell them everything Will and I had talked about, which, when you came down to it, wasn't all that much. Still, I had stayed up way too late after he left, wishing I hadn't cut him off when he tried to steer the conversation in a personal direction.

"Well, he must know about bones and all from his job," Mam said. "I would think he saw lots of bodies when he was with the sheriff's in Columbia."

"He used to, when he worked robbery and homicide," I said. "But he's been doing field training and administration the last few years. He knows some forensics, but most of it gets taken care of by the crime-scene people if they need them, like those investigators on TV. But we agreed that whatever it was, it wasn't real new. It sure looked old to me. Anyway, he took it to his place for safekeeping until he can show it to the medical examiner. If it's human, they'll have to send it to the state lab."

"I swear, that phone hasn't stopped ringing all day," said Margaret Ann, getting up from the kitchen table. "But where did I leave it? It must be in the den."

"That interfering Myrtle Finch from Mama's bridge club called right as we were leaving this morning," Bonnie said. "Said she was so sorry she hadn't been at the service, but that she'd had to carry Dabney to a doctor's appointment in Charleston to see some specialist. 'Course, what she really wanted to know was if we had made a ship-to-shore call to tell the folks."

"I hope you set her straight," I said. "She's a great one for wanting to know everybody's business. She probably knows more than we do about what happened at Pinckney, and we were there. Maybe she doesn't know that, though."

But I wasn't hopeful. Too many people had been at the service yesterday, and it hadn't been out of love for Bradford Bentley. Pinckney Plantation wasn't just a draw for tourists—or "guests," as Cissy had informed us Miss Augusta now wanted to call them. Pinckney and Miss Augusta were Indigo Island institutions. Anything that happened at the plantation was news, from rumors that Miss Augusta might raise admission prices by fifty cents to her plans to stage a history pageant on the grounds come summer. A fatal accident was the most exciting thing to hit Indigo since Miss Augusta had given Pinck permission to build a few spec houses with Ray Simmons on the plantation's far creek. Just wait until the islanders figured out that Bentley's accident might not have been an accident.

"Mam talked to Myrtle, asked her all about Dabney's diverticulitis," Bonnie said. "That kept her going. That woman can talk a blue streak."

"Speaking of blue streaks, did you see Miss Rachel's hair at the service yesterday? It's practically the color of Cissy's tour dress. If we go over to Aunt Cora's later, she'll probably come over when she sees our car. She's another nosy one."

"You got that right," Margaret Ann said, sailing into the kitchen. "And it's a good thing, too. Where are my car keys? And why are y'all sitting there like two bumps on a log? That was Miss Rachel. We need to high-tail it over to Aunt Cora's. Miss Rachel said Will's patrol car has been parked in her driveway all morning, which explains why Aunt Cora wasn't at church. I thought maybe she went to the Presbyterians this morning."

"Why didn't Miss Rachel call us before?" Bonnie asked, shrugging into her jacket and holding the door for me.

I ducked under her arm. "Because the line was busy with

Dabney's durned diverticulitis!"

Will's cruiser was still in Aunt Cora's driveway. Mam almost took out a camellia bush as she parked in front of the house, one of only a handful of brick ranches on an island where building permits and flood insurance required homes to be up off the ground. But this cul-de-sac off Sandy Creek Road was on a high point in a stand of tall pines.

"I still don't understand why Aunt Cora didn't call us herself," Mam said. "Or Will should have called you, Bonnie. You're a lawyer."

"Mam, can't you get it straight that I'm an environmental lawyer, not a criminal lawyer? I deal with dead plants, not dead people. And aren't you the one who watches *Law & Order* all the time? Since when do the police call a lawyer unless it's a prosecutor? Besides, Will may not even know I'm a lawyer."

"He knows," I said. "I told him last night you had to come down here for a last-minute meeting, so those papers could be filed before New Year's." It had been my contribution to the conversation at one of those points when the silence between Will and me had gone on too long.

"Well, Aunt Cora should have called me," Mam said. "I am her favorite."

"Oh, let's not go there, Miss High and Mighty Matthews," Bonnie said. "Aunt Cora doesn't play favorites. You just happen to see her more."

"Shush," I said, going up the front-porch steps. "Miss Rachel likely can hear the two of you from across the street. And I know she's watching, 'cause I saw the curtains twitch."

Aunt Cora's door opened just as I reached out to thump the

brass lion's head door knocker, and I found myself thumping Will's chest instead. Bonnie crashed into the back of me as Mam crashed into her, and then my nose was scrunched against Will's leather jacket. I jerked back and stepped on Bonnie.

Will reached out to steady me. "Whoa there, ladies," he said. "One at a time."

"In your dreams, Will McLeod," Bonnie said, smiling sweetly.

My cousin always has had a way with words. I would have to remember to tell her how good her hair looked today.

"We're here to see Aunt Cora," I said, regaining some measure of composure.

"Where is she?" said Mam. "What have you done with her?"

"He hasn't done anything to me," Aunt Cora said from somewhere behind Will.

"Now, Aunt Cora, you know you don't have to say a word to him," Bonnie said in her most lawyerly voice. "Has he read you your rights?"

"Read me my rights? Land's sake. You girls watch too much TV. All we did was eat some lemon pie, and I helped Will with some little details about who all was at Pinckney the other afternoon." She nodded toward the kitchen. "There's still some pie left, if you'd like to sit a spell and visit. Bonnie, you come sit here by me and tell me about those two little boys of yours. Margaret Ann, there's a fresh pitcher of tea in the icebox, and the pie's right there on the table. Lindsey, you can show Will out. It was nice to see you, son. You tell your mama I asked after her."

I looked at my aunt. Her arm was still in the sling, but she didn't act as if it was bothering her. Aunt Cora was good at hiding things, though. What had she and Will been talking about? Not much got by her, that was for sure. If you wanted to know something about island history, she, Miss Augusta, and Miss

Maudie were the leading authorities.

I followed Will onto the porch. "What are you doing here?" I said, careful not to raise my voice. I didn't want Miss Rachel—or Aunt Cora, for that matter—to hear me. "You can't possibly think that sweet little old lady had anything to do with Bradford Bentley getting himself killed."

Will grinned, his eyes crinkling. "Now, *sweet* is not a word most folks would use to describe Cora Hudson," he said. "I was in the post office last week when she came stomping in and read Grady Rivers the riot act for taking up two parking spaces. And I've heard her at the Piggly Wiggly when someone gets in the express lane with too many items in their cart."

"All right, so she can be a little impatient at times. Or a lot impatient. No one in our family suffers fools gladly, and Grady Rivers is at least two kinds of fool." I looked at him sternly, or tried to. It's hard to be intimidating when you aren't much more than five feet tall and your nose turns up. "But that's not the point. I'm sure Aunt Cora doesn't know anything that can help you."

"You might be surprised at what your aunt knows," Will said. He was serious now. "Listen, Lindsey, you and I really need to talk sometime. But not about this case. I've probably told you more than I should have already. Like about that bone. You haven't said anything about it to anyone, have you?"

I stared at my black boots. There was a scuff mark on the right one.

"You told Margaret Ann and Bonnie, didn't you?"

"I didn't tell them about Cissy finding it with Jimmy," I said in my defense. "And I didn't tell them you're pretty sure it's human. Just that it might be."

"Lindsey, that bone probably doesn't have anything to do with the case, but I'd just as soon no one know about it. I told Jimmy not to say anything, and for him to tell Cissy. Now, I want you to tell your cousins that it looks like it's an old bone from a deer or a mule, and then I don't want to hear another word about it. And I don't want to hear that y'all have been playing detective. This is an official investigation into a suspicious death, and if I need any help, it won't be from amateurs."

"You seem to forget that I'm a reporter, Will, and Bonnie's a lawyer," I said. "And Margaret Ann knows everybody on this island, white, black, brown, or purple. You haven't been living here that long this time around. We might actually be of help to you."

"I seriously doubt it, but if I do need help, I'll ask for it. Until then, just stay out of it. Enjoy the holidays, or what's left of them." He started down the steps, then stopped. "Lindsey, I do want to talk, you know, about other stuff, when there's a chance—"

"You had your chance a long time ago," I interrupted. "Don't hold your breath now."

I shut Aunt Cora's front door firmly. Maybe a little too firmly. I could see the curtains moving at Miss Rachel's.

I found Aunt Cora, Bonnie, and Mam sitting around the dinette. A slice of lemon pie was waiting for me on a Blue Willow dessert plate next to a glass of tea.

"Did you see on the TV where all those folks in Arkansas are without power 'cause of that storm?" Aunt Cora said. "Some of them don't even have water, 'cause the pipes all froze. They're calling it 'Holiday on Ice.' "

"I think it's just supposed to be rainy here tonight," Mam offered. "Might be cold by New Year's, though."

"That's just two days away," said Bonnie.

I ate my pie. I could tell from Mam's and Bonnie's faces that

Aunt Cora hadn't told them anything important. She obviously wasn't giving anything away today, including the recipe for the pie, which I had been after for years. Still, I had to try.

"Aunt Cora," I said, "about this pie . . ."

"Now, Lindsey," she said. "I've told you the recipe is on the Argo Cornstarch box."

"But you must add something to it. Some secret ingredient. Mine never tastes like this."

"Or mine," Bonnie and Mam echoed.

"No, girls. I am not Colonel Sanders. No secrets here."

" 'No secrets here,' huh?" I said when we were in the car. "I'm guessing Aunt Cora didn't tell you a thing."

"Not squat," said Mam.

"She knows something, though," Bonnie said. "Every time I started to mention the historical society or Miss Augusta, she just changed the subject. What did Will tell you just now? Does he know anything more about the bone?"

"He said for me to tell you that it came from a big deer or a mule."

"Gosh, I was really hoping it was a clue," Mam said.

"Wait a minute," Bonnie said. "Say again what you just said."

"I heard her," Mam said. "Will said it wasn't human."

"No, that's not what she said, is it, Lindsey?"

I smiled. "Very good, cuz. Will said for me to tell you that it came from a big deer or a mule."

"Aha!" said Mam. "I get it. So it is human."

"I think he thinks it is, but he wouldn't say. And I don't know whether it's even connected with this case or not. He did have the guest register from Pinckney with him, so I guess he really was just asking Aunt Cora who was where at what time."

"Alibis," Mam said knowingly. "Aunt Cora doesn't have one. Evidently, she'd gone to relieve Beth at the gift shop and lock up, but Beth had already gone."

"So you did get something from her," I said. "Will just told me he'd already said too much, and for us to stop playing detective."

"I take it we're not listening to him," Bonnie said.

"Of course not," I said. "But I'm not sure what we do next. Aunt Cora's a walking history book of this island. I was counting on her. It's Sunday, and both the library and the historical museum are closed."

"You're forgetting someone," Mam said, driving past the road to her house and pointing the car inland, toward the middle of the island. "Let's go see Miss Maudie."

I like Middle House as much as about any house on the island. It's old, maybe even older than Pinckney, but not nearly as big. Just a wide, white frame house with a wraparound porch. In the spring, giant pink azaleas—the kind that won't grow in sandy beach soil—practically hide it from the rutted dirt road that winds off the highway past the Presbyterian church on its way toward Crab Creek. Even on a late-December day, with the ground more brown than green and bare tree limbs etched against the pearly sky, the house looked welcoming, the moss festooning the oak trees waving us up the drive.

"I'm not so sure this is a good idea," Bonnie said. "You know, she won't half understand what we're saying, unless she's had that hearing aid fixed."

"I think she did," Mam said. "At least it wasn't making that bird sound at the funeral, and she wasn't fiddling with it like usual. I was sitting right behind her and that big old hat of hers. Couldn't hardly see around it. Besides, she saw you at the funeral, and her feelings will be hurt if we don't drop by for a visit. You give her that banana nut bread I took out the freezer. I was going to give it to Aunt Cora and forgot to take it in. I made it back in October, but I think it's still good."

"She probably wouldn't know the difference," Bonnie said. "But I'm glad you brought it. Maybe she'll offer us some of it, instead of that Whitman's Sampler she's had since before we were born."

"It's not that old," I said. "Maybe before Cissy was born."

"Whatever," Bonnie said. "You know, she takes that name *Sampler* literally. She takes pieces out and tastes them, and if she doesn't like them, she puts them back. Be careful. Anything with caramel or nuts in it likely has bite marks."

"That's because she doesn't want to pull out a tooth or break one," Mam said. "Just remember, she's going to be a good source of information for us. She and Miss Augusta and Aunt Cora were all girls together. They've known each other forever."

"Like us," I said.

"Yep," said Bonnie. "And just think what all we have on each other."

Mam laughed, and I nodded. But I wondered how much, if anything, they knew or suspected about me and Will.

"Whooee, whooee!" Mam called out as she rang the doorbell and knocked on the screen door at the same time. "Miss Maudie, are you home?"

"I can hear the TV," said Bonnie.

"So can everybody on Indigo Island," I said. "Knock again."

"She sees us," Mam said.

Through the side glass by the door, we could see Miss Maudie in her print dress and red shawl doddering toward us. It took her a minute to unbolt the door and turn the skeleton key in the lock.

"Well, look who's here!" Miss Maudie reached up and grabbed Mam's head and landed a big smack on her ear. I reached out to give the old lady a hug before she could get to my ear, but Bonnie wasn't so lucky.

"Bonnie was in town, so we thought we'd come by for a minute!" Mam shouted over the deafening noise of the TV. "I hope it's not an inconvenience!"

"Goodness gracious, as if I had anything important to do," Miss Maudie said. "I had the TV on, but it's just football, football, football." She picked up the remote and turned the sound down to a dull roar. "They even had football on Friday afternoon when I wanted to watch my programs. Guess they're going to make us wait till next week to find out about Erica's daughter. Now, where are my manners? What can I get you girls? How about some tea and a piece of fruitcake?"

I tried not to look at the others. Miss Maudie's fruitcakes were as infamous as her Whitman's Sampler. Legend had it that she gave one for Christmas years ago and the recipient broke his big toe when he tripped over it reaching to change a light bulb on his tree. Reportedly, he used it for a doorstop till spring, when some raccoons finally succeeded in carrying it off.

"We brought you some of Mam's nut bread," Bonnie said, handing over the foil-wrapped package tied with red ribbon. "But you save it for later. We just had some pie with Aunt Cora."

"How is Cora?" Miss Maudie said, settling back in her recliner and pulling the shawl around her.

Bonnie and I sat in the armchairs on either side of the old gas heater that stood in front of what had once been the fireplace. No central heating here. My right leg was about to burn up, and my left one was turning into an icicle. In about five minutes, Bonnie and I would have to stand up and switch places. Mam had grabbed the couch beside Miss Maudie and wrapped herself in a hideous brown-and-orange afghan.

"Oh, Aunt Cora's just fine," Mam said. "But I think she's worried about Mr. Bentley's death and how Miss Augusta is taking it."

Miss Maudie made a little clucking sound. "I declare."

"It is a sad business," I ventured. "Did you know Mr. Bentley well?"

"Oh, no," Miss Maudie said. "He came out here once with Augusta back when he first came to Indigo, but I only saw him once or twice after that, at historical-society meetings. I know Augusta thought he hung the moon, although Cora didn't much care for him."

"Why was that?" Bonnie asked.

"Oh, it was that book he was writing about Indigo. That's what started all the recent trouble between Augusta and Cora. He applied for some more grant money from the society for research, and Cora didn't want him to have it. Said his book was too narrow, all about the Pinckneys and not enough about the rest of the island. That's always been a sore point between Augusta and Cora anyways."

"How so?" I asked.

"Oh, you know, we all grew up here together—Foxes and Framptons, Hudsons and Pinckneys, Riverses and Lindseys. The

Matthews, too." She nodded at Mam. "Those families have been on the island since way back when. The Seabrooks came over here from Edisto, and some of the Mikells. My mama's people were the Hiotts up at Round O. But the point is that we are all part of the island's history, and so are the black families—the Washingtons and Singletons and Manigaults. For most of us, it makes no difference, it's just the way things are. Indigo's home. It didn't matter when Augusta, Cora, and I were girls. Everyone was land-poor. But then some aunt of Augusta's gave her some money to go to boarding school in Richmond, and when she came back, she decided that the Pinckneys were like—what do you call it?—the fine families of Virginia."

"Something like that," Bonnie said.

She poked me, and we exchanged places. Now I was sitting next to the fake silver Christmas tree Miss Maudie had decorated with an assortment of ornaments. Large purple satin balls from a holiday bazaar hung next to homemade flour-and-paste gingerbread men no doubt donated by her great-grandchildren. The kids had been down Christmas Day—all the tiny, plastic-wrapped candy canes were gone, except from the tallest branches near a lopsided foil star.

"Well, now, Cora has never been one to put up with airs and graces," Miss Maudie said, "and she told Augusta that the Pinckneys weren't any better than anybody else on Indigo. And that was their first falling out. But this is a small place, and after a while, things got patched up. It might have been when I married Mr. Frampton, God rest his soul, and they were both in my wedding. And it wasn't too long after that when Cora and Carl Ed got together, and Augusta met Carter Townsend through a cousin at the Citadel. She wasn't on the island all that much after that. She didn't really come back here till Carter died and she got the idea to turn Pinckney into a tourist attraction. She thought that Bradford's book would help bring in more tourists, really put it on the map, like Boone Hall."

Well, Bradford's book wouldn't, that was for sure, seeing as how he hadn't finished it. But his death might. Of course, it had taken both a murder and a book to bring the throngs to Mercer House in Savannah.

"And then I think Augusta liked Bradford because he knew Julia," Miss Maudie said.

Bonnie, Mam, and I looked at one another. This was news to us. Julia was Miss Augusta's only daughter, who had died more than twenty-five years ago in a car wreck in Canada. She'd run off from college with a war resister and stayed.

"That was a sad business, too," Miss Maudie clucked.

We knew she was referring not only to Julia's death but also to the fact that her father had cut her off without a word. I don't think I'd ever seen Julia but about once or twice, if that. She was a teenager when we were babies, and being a military family, they'd moved every few years. 'Course, it was because her father was military that there was a rift between them during Vietnam. What might have been just ordinary teenage rebellion had flared with the times. Mam and I had thought it was romantic when we were in junior high and heard about Julia running off with a handsome draft dodger. But now we both knew it must have hurt Miss Augusta to no end, not being able to reconcile her husband and daughter before they both died, Julia in the crash that also killed her boyfriend and Carter from a stroke not long after.

"Bradford Bentley knew Julia?" Bonnie asked.

"Seems he met her up in Washington when he was in college,

before she went and broke her mama and daddy's heart, running off with that other fellow." Miss Maudie nodded. "That was a time, all right."

"Yes'm," Mam said.

I could tell that, like Bonnie and me, she was wondering just how well Bradford knew Julia. And here was another avenue to explore. Had Bradford gone to Vietnam? He'd have been about the right age. Maybe we needed to find out more about Mr. Bradford Bentley than just what he'd been doing on Indigo the last few months.

"Oh, girls," Miss Maudie said. "I got to talking so much I forgot my manners. Margaret Ann, reach back over there by that little Christmas tree. I've got a Whitman's Sampler."

chapter seven

Oh, Deer!

"You are such a liar, Bonnie Lynn!" Margaret Ann said. "Imagine telling Miss Maudie that you of all people had developed an allergy to chocolate. That's going to come back to haunt you the next time she sees you scarfing a brownie or some chocolate pound cake."

"Well, at least I'm not picking gnawed caramel out of my teeth," Bonnie said. "I've only got this one crown, and I don't want to lose it. They cost a fortune. What did you get, anyway?"

"Vanilla cream, I think," Mam said. "Lindsey grabbed the bird's eggs."

"I like candy-coated almonds," I defended. " 'Course, there's no telling how old those were." I'd sucked the pink and blue shells off and then slipped the two nuts in a pocket in my jeans. I'd throw them in the yard and let some squirrel have at 'em.

"Speaking of old, do y'all remember how much older Julia was than us?" Bonnie asked. "Was she the same age as Bradford? You know, we need to find out more about him. First, though, I could do with some real food."

"We'll go see what there is to snack on," Mam said, turning into her drive. J. T.'s truck was there. He no doubt was watching football. "You coming, Lindsey?"

"Thanks, but I think I'll go home, maybe take a nap," I said. "I'll call you later."

It was only midafternoon, but it felt later. The sky had clouded up even more, silver darkening to gray. And I realized I was hungry. All I'd eaten today was lemon pie and that little bit of candy, not having had the luxury of the bacon and waffles Margaret Ann traditionally fixed on Sunday morning. J. T. always teased her, saying it was just her way out of cooking a big Sunday dinner. Driving home, I mentally went through the contents of Mama's refrigerator and freezer. How long would it take to thaw out that homemade vegetable soup?

Too long, I decided, and abruptly swung the CR-V into the almost empty parking lot of the Beachside Café, one of the few restaurants on Indigo that stayed open all year. I needed to decipher the day's events and put my thoughts in order, and I couldn't do that on an empty stomach.

But as I pushed open the glass door with "Merry Christmas" sprayed on it with fake snow, I realized putting my thoughts in order wasn't going to happen with Will sitting at the counter.

He paused with his fork halfway to his mouth. "Well, hello, Lindsey."

"Hey, Will," I said, silently cursing. His cruiser wasn't outside. He must be in his own truck. I chose a booth near the back and sat facing away from him, hoping he'd take the hint that I wanted to be alone.

He didn't. I was intently staring at the old red vinyl menu when he slipped in across from me, bringing his coffee cup with him.

"You planning on ordering breakfast this time of day?" he asked.

"Huh?"

"That's the breakfast menu you're looking at."

"Some people eat breakfast any time of day, I'll have you know."

"Not here. The café doesn't serve it after ten." He raised his head and called to Eula as she came out the swinging kitchen door. "Eula, will you please bring Lindsey here a Coke and a burger with everything but onions? Oh, and a large order of fries."

"Make that a small order of fries, please," I said, turning my head. "Did you have a big Christmas, Eula?"

"It was pretty big," she said, coming over to refill Will's coffee and give me my Coke in a tall plastic tumbler. "Tiny's family came over for the day from Little Britton. Medium or medium-well?"

"Medium, please."

I took my time opening my straw. Will sipped his coffee.

"So, what have you been doing since I saw you at Cora's?" he asked.

"Not much. We drove out to Middle House so Bonnie could see Miss Maudie."

Will's eyes narrowed. "Oh, really?"

"Yes, really." I decided it was my turn. "And what have *you* been doing?"

"This and that."

"Find out anything?"

"Maybe. Did you?"

"What?"

"Find out anything?"

"Maybe."

This wasn't getting us anywhere. I looked out the window and saw Grady Rivers drive by. His beagle, Daisy, was riding shotgun.

"Do you have a dog?" I asked Will. During high school, he'd had a black Lab called Ace.

"Not right now," he said. "I was thinking maybe I'd get Jimmy a Lab puppy for graduation. What about you?"

"Just Peaches the cat at the moment," I said. "I had this great golden, but she died a couple of years ago. I want another dog, now that I'm full-time with the magazine and don't have to travel so much. But I'm not sure I want to go through the puppy years again."

"Dogs are good company." Will set his coffee cup down. "Lindsey . . ."

Thankfully, my lunch arrived. Eula pulled the squeeze bottles of ketchup and mustard out from behind the salt and pepper, hefting them to make sure they weren't empty. "Anything else? More coffee, Will?"

"No, thank you."

"Okay, I'll be back in the kitchen if anybody needs something."

Will pushed the ketchup toward me and stuck the mustard back in its place. That he remembered I liked extra ketchup and not mustard surprised me. Of course, I remembered that he liked the exact opposite. But that was different. Girls remembered little things. Guys were supposed to be oblivious. That Will wasn't, even after all this time, gave me something to chew on besides the hamburger.

Will's mind seemed to be going in the same direction, because he waited until my mouth was full to launch the conversation he'd been wanting to have since he saw me on the porch at Pinckney. "Seeing you there with those fries and that ketchup on your chin brings back a lot of memories," he said. "Remember that burger joint on Franklin Street?"

I swallowed, then dabbed at my chin with my napkin. "They tore it down," I said, not looking at him. I drank some Coke. "A long time ago."

"Too bad," Will said. "I liked it a lot." I could tell he was looking at me, but I continued to arrange the fries around the perimeter of my plate. His voice softened. "I liked you a lot, too. More than liked."

What was I supposed to say to that? Yes, you liked me a lot, loved me even, but you went home the weekend after Valentine's and married Darlene? Yes, she was pregnant, which meant you slept with her over Christmas break, when supposedly you were breaking up with her? And you conveniently forgot to mention that part when we rode back to Chapel Hill together after New Year's, when you told me it was all over between the two of you? And you never even called to say you were married, so Margaret Ann excitedly told me in a long-distance phone call on a Sunday night when I was trying to study for a French lit test while wondering why you hadn't shown up yet?

" '*Il pleure dans mon coeur.*' " I looked at Will. It rains in my heart.

"What?"

"It's French," I said. "Like *C'est la vie.* That's life. It was a long time ago. Things change, people change. *Qué será, será*. That's Spanish." I waved a French fry, trying to be nonchalant. "Whatever will be, will be." I couldn't seem to stop talking in clichés. Maybe I even believed them.

But I knew one way to get Will off this unwanted stroll down memory lane: "Did you know that Bradford Bentley knew Julia Townsend?"

He sat up straight. I smiled and ate another bite. I could tell this was news to him.

"How well did he know Julia?"

"Don't know," I said. "But it kind of makes you wonder how well anyone around here knew him. Seems to me that you need to know the victim before you can find out who killed him."

"Lindsey, I don't need your advice on how to investigate a crime. I've already told you to keep that cute little nose of yours out of this. You and your cousins seem to forget that this isn't a game of Clue. It's not a case of Colonel Mustard in the drawing room with a candlestick."

"Could it have been a candlestick? He didn't just hit his head on the floor, did he?"

"Lindsey, what did I just tell you? This isn't a game."

"I never said it was. I'm just being a good reporter and asking questions of local law enforcement."

"Well, you can tell all your *Perfect Pet* readers that I have no comment."

I decided I was finished. I took a last swig of Coke and reached for the check.

Will's hand landed on mine and stayed there. "I'll take care of this," he said.

"No, I can do it," I said. "And would you please take your

hand off? There are other people in here."

In fact, an older man with a weather-beaten face, work boots, and a John Deere cap was heading for the jukebox in the corner behind us. He nodded at Will, who still hadn't moved his hand.

I was expecting to hear a country song—George Strait, or maybe even Willie Nelson. But instead the familiar, melancholy strains of Ella Fitzgerald singing "Mood Indigo" filled the café.

Listening to the song a minute, I knew what to say to Will. "You know, Ellington wrote the music first, and the words didn't come till a lot later. I heard them talking about it on NPR, one of the great songs of the century. Seems Ellington said he had in mind a young girl sitting in a window—a girl waiting on a boy. She was sitting there in that window, just thinking about that boy, waiting on him, wondering where he was. But he didn't come. He never came."

Will moved his hand. Mine felt cold as I picked up the check and took out my wallet to leave a tip. But Will had already put a couple dollars on the table.

"At least let me do this," he said.

"All right," I said. I didn't want to talk anymore.

"When can I see you again?" Will asked.

I slid out of the booth and looked at him. "Mood Indigo" was ending. "No comment," I said.

It had started to rain while I was in the café, a combination of mist and drizzle that made the beach seem as if it were shrouded in a cloud. "*Il pleure dans mon coeur.*" I hadn't thought of that poem in ages.

Ages. I knew one way to find out how old Julia Townsend would be if she were still alive. I hung a left out of the café and drove toward Pinckney. After the causeway over the marsh, the main road twisted through the center of the island like a black snake. "Bridge Ices Before Road," read the sign as I came around the curve near Crab Creek. A couple of cars and trucks passed me on their way to the beach, but it looked like most people were staying in on this Sunday afternoon. Smoke drifted from the chimney of the old manse next to the Presbyterian church.

I turned right on Magnolia Bluff Road and slowed to make a left into the drive toward Pinckney. The wrought-iron gate between the two brick pillars covered in creeping fig was closed. I pulled up next to the metal security box, which was practically hidden by pittosporum bushes that needed trimming. The box had been updated—it now looked like a computer screen—but I was counting on the entry code not having changed. Otherwise, I'd be out of luck, since Miss Augusta was spending the weekend in Charleston after the memorial service yesterday. I punched in the four numbers and held my breath.

The gate slowly swung open, and I headed up the drive. Looking in the rearview mirror, I was reassured when the gate automatically closed behind me. No need for anyone to know I was here. I turned left off the main drive, heading toward the old chapel and graveyard.

The rain was now just a fine mist—perfect for poking around a cemetery if you wanted to look for ghosts. I didn't. There were too many real-life reminders of the past showing up as it was. Would the blue of my jeans satisfy the old Gullah superstition about the color and keep away Marietta's haints? I certainly hoped so.

Leaves and twigs crunched under my feet as I opened the old iron gate separating the Pinckney plot from the other grave sites.

A tall granite marker inscribed with the family name stood in the center, smaller monuments and headstones laid out in squares around it. The newer graves were near the front, and here was the one I was looking for, a polished pink marble slab: *Julia Pinckney Townsend*. Below her name were the words *Beloved Daughter*, and below that her dates: *August 8, 1946-November 12, 1971*.

Let's see. That meant she'd have been just a few years older than Bradford. And she was only twenty-five when she died. I shivered, as if someone had walked over my own grave. I stared at the marker. I had a vague recollection of an auburn-haired teen helping Margaret Ann and me look for Easter eggs. It was one of my earliest memories. Had that been Julia? I couldn't remember ever seeing any photographs of her at Pinckney. Maybe her father had burned them, or Miss Augusta had hidden them so he wouldn't find them.

But there was no doubt she loved Julia. And thought of her often, every time she opened the gate to Pinckney by punching in 8846. *August 8, 1946.*

I always forget how dark the island roads can be, especially in December, when night falls so early. The cold, damp air seemed to seep into my bones, even with the heat on.

Suddenly, there was a blur of movement in front of my headlights. I slammed on the brakes, recognizing the arched shape of a deer even though it was gone in an instant. The back of the CR-V swerved on the wet pavement but held as I pulled off the road, gripping the steering wheel hard.

Geez. That was close. I took a deep breath, leaning my head against the steering wheel. My arms were trembling. At least I hadn't hit the poor deer and wouldn't have to go looking for an injured Bambi that would have to be put out of its misery.

My stomach was reacting to the very thought. Or maybe it was the adrenaline. I hit the button to open the window, welcoming the chill dampness now. My headlights cut into the darkness, illuminating another bend in the road. And something else.

An overflowing black garbage bag? I squinted at the shadowy shape. Damn. I retrieved the flashlight from the glove compartment, hoping the batteries were still good. They were. Climbing out, I directed the beam over the wet leaves and through the naked trees by the roadside. Whatever it was lay about ten feet away. I waded through the sticky grass.

"Please don't be Bambi, please don't be Bambi," I chanted to myself.

No, not Bambi, unless he had started carrying a Pinckney Plantation canvas tote. I could see the familiar blue-purple logo on a khaki bag gripped in the gloved hand of a crumpled figure lying face down. I couldn't see much else because the light was jerking up and down in my hand.

"Breathe deeply," I whispered to myself. "You can do this."

Oh, God, please tell me this person's not dead, too.

"I see dead people," I said, hysteria starting to take over.

Really, I was not good in these situations. Where was Mam when I needed her? I leaned over for a closer look.

"Sir, are you all right?"

Stupid question. My flashlight found black-and-gray hair matted with leaves and mud. Or was it blood?

My stomach was threatening to come up my throat. I ran back for my cell phone and hit 911.

No signal. Crap. That's one of the things about Indigo. Cell phones often don't work in the low-lying inland areas. There are dead spots. Right, *dead.* Perfect.

I hit the button that unlocked the rear door, swung it open, and used the floor of the trunk to boost myself onto the CR-V's slippery roof. I didn't dare stand up, but maybe I was high enough to get a tower signal. I didn't try 911 again, though. Mam was lots closer than the dispatcher.

"Mam, it's me. Call 911. I can't get it on this cell phone. Can you hear me? Oh, Lord, I think he's dead."

"Who's dead? Lindsey, where are you? And what are you talking about?"

"I don't know who he is. He's lying here. I'm out on the King's Road, not too far from the curve after White Oak but before the little bridge. Call 911 on your regular phone, then call me back. Oh, I think I see a car coming! I'll try and flag them down. Hurry."

"Lindsey, Lindsey, don't you hang up—"

I waved the flashlight at the oncoming car, yelling, "Stop! Help! Stop!" Surely, whoever it was would see the light or hear me. I was loud enough to wake the dead. *Dead.* Mam was right. We used that word entirely too much without thinking.

The car pulled over. Oh, good, it was Will's cruiser. No . . .

"Olivia! Come help. I'm so glad you're here. There's somebody lying right off the road up there."

My cell phone rang.

"Lindsey, what's happening? I called 911, and EMS is on its way. We're on our way, too. Bonnie's driving. We're pulling out the drive now. You just stay here on the line with me, and I'll talk you through this. Who is it? Don't you go and throw up before you find out."

My considerate cousin.

"Hang on," I said.

My flashlight found Olivia kneeling beside the man. "EMS is coming!" I yelled. "What do you want me to do?"

She looked up at me, and tears were coming down her cheeks. "Don't you think you've done enough already?"

"What?" I said.

I could hear Mam's voice from my phone. Sitting up there on the roof, I could see that Olivia had turned the man over. Only it wasn't a man. It was Marietta. She must have been walking to the Sunday-night prayer meeting at Mount Zion.

I started to clamber down.

"You stay right where you are, Lindsey Fox," Olivia barked, shining her strong flashlight square in my face. "You've hurt my auntie enough already. I just hope you haven't killed her."

"Killed her?" My voice squeaked. "Me, no. Olivia, it wasn't me. There was this deer, and . . ." I gave up.

Olivia turned her attention to Marietta. Margaret Ann was still yapping on my cell phone. I heard sirens in the distance. Déjà vu all over again. I lifted the phone to my ear.

"Slow down, Bonnie, or we're going to end up in the marsh, and then where—"

I cut Mam off in midsentence. "It's Marietta, but she's not dead, leastways I don't think so. Only Olivia thinks I ran her down, and I didn't, it was the deer. Oh, dammit to hell!" I was starting to cry. "Y'all come on, everybody else is. It'll be like Old Home Week." I hiccuped.

Margaret Ann was asking if I had my AAA card, 'cause if not, J. T. knew a good bail bondsman. But I tuned her out. Obviously, she, too, thought I was guilty of running down an old lady.

The rescue squad, lights flashing, pulled up in the middle of the road. And Will was right behind. Oh, great. My hero. My alibi.

"Mam," I said firmly. "I'm hanging up now, and I'm turning off the phone. I think I'm going to be sick."

And I was.

chapter eight

We Three Snoops, or "Keep Out" Doesn't Mean Us

"Isn't that the tackiest thing you've ever heard?"

"I don't know," I said. "I haven't heard it yet."

Mam had the morning paper spread out on her kitchen table, looking to see if there was anything about last night's hit-and-run on Indigo. I'd told her it was too late to have made the regional edition—besides which, no one was dead. Thankfully, Marietta was going to be all right, though she'd be in the hospital for several days. Mam had phoned me with that news at the crack of dawn. "She has a concussion," she'd informed me. "And she doesn't remember anything about last night."

I remembered too much, including losing my lunch in the ditch just as Will arrived on the scene. After the ambulance left, Mam had driven me home in the CR-V, with Bonnie following.

Mam had suggested some Pepto-Bismol, Bonnie a slug of Daddy's Johnny Walker Red. I'd suggested that a little Gatorade and a lot of sleep would suit me just fine, and I'd see them in the morning.

"What's tacky?" I asked now.

"This woman," Mam said. She tapped her finger on a story on the front of the local section. "You know, they passed that new zoning law over on Edisto Island about how houses on the beach can only be so big. Evidently, she and her husband were planning to build some huge monstrosity practically the size of Pinckney. Anyway, she said—and I quote—'The people here are just jealous because we have the money to do this and they don't.' "

"She actually said that?"

"Yep. Can you believe it? I bet she wears white shoes in the winter."

"And diamonds during the day."

"Too tacky for words," we said in unison, grinning.

"Not exactly the way to endear yourself to your new neighbors either," I added. "Speaking of which, the Caldwells are coming back from Florida today, so they'll be at the Simmons' party tonight."

Mam raised her eyebrows. "How do you know that?"

"Luis Rivera told me."

"You don't know Luis Rivera." Her tone was accusatory.

"Yes, I do," I said, enjoying the moment. It isn't often I can scoop Mam on island news. "I met him on the beach this morning."

I saw his footprints before I saw him.

The tracks surprised me as I came up over the dune onto the beach, where a brisk breeze ruffled the whitecaps on the gray-green water. The sky was pale blue and streaked with thin white clouds. This time of year, this early in the morning, I was used to having this end of the beach to myself. Not that there was much beach at the moment. The tide was going out, leaving a narrow strip of wet sand speckled with shell fragments.

Whoever he was, he was wearing Reeboks. The word stood out clearly among the cross-hatchings on each print. My eyes followed the prints to the right, toward where the beach tapered off as the island curved into the mouth of the river.

I saw him then. He was at the water's edge about fifty yards away, his back to me, looking out toward Pine Island. Navy nylon jacket, blue jeans, black hair. A stranger.

I couldn't decide what to do. If I turned and walked to the left as usual, heading toward The Point, he'd be behind me. Somehow, I didn't like that idea.

Get a grip, I told myself. He was talking on a cell phone. A lot of people came out on the beach so they could get a clear signal.

Going right was silly. That would bring me up behind him almost immediately. Of course, I could turn around and go back to the house, but I really wanted to stretch my legs and clear away the cobwebs before going over to Mam's.

Oh, this was stupid. Why did he have to be here on my beach?

I saw the dog then. The color of sea oats, he came over the crest of a dune and sniffed the air. Then he saw me. Tail wagging, he splashed through a shallow pool left by the outgoing tide, fifty-plus pounds of fur heading toward me.

"Pablo, stop!"

The dog—some sort of yellow Lab mix—kept coming.

"Pablo!" the man called. "Pablo, here!"

"Hey, boy," I said, kneeling. "Good dog."

A black-spotted tongue licked my hand. He must have some chow in him.

"He won't hurt you," said the man, coming up to us. He slipped a check chain over the wiggling dog's head. "He just gets excited."

"I can see that," I said, standing. I could also see his owner. Chiseled features, cleft chin, eyes as dark as his short-cropped hair. It was unfair for a guy to have such long lashes. He was maybe my age, give or take a couple of years.

The dog was leaping between the two of us.

"He's not mine," the man said. "I mean, he is now, but he belonged to a friend who couldn't keep him. I told her I'd find him a home. He's been to obedience school, but I can't always get him to listen."

The dog was pawing at me, trying to get my attention.

"Pablo, sit!" I commanded.

The dog sat.

"Good dog," I said, patting his head. "It's in the voice," I explained. "You have to say it like you mean it. Also, if he belonged to a woman, he's probably used to her voice. . . ." My own trailed off lamely. I didn't want to sound like a know-it-all. I took a breath. "Hey. Lindsey Fox. My folks live right there." I gestured behind me.

"Luis Rivera," he said.

"Oh," I said. "You're with the Caldwells."

He looked surprised.

"It's a small island. Word gets around."

"Yes, it does." He finally smiled, and the effect was devastating. Hadn't Mam said he was single? It didn't seem possible. "You would be one of the women who, um . . ."

"Found the body. Yes, me and my cousin. Did you know Mr. Bentley?"

"I'd met him. He was a friend of the Caldwells."

"I didn't see them at the service. Are they out of town?"

The dog was still sitting there, looking at me alertly, as if he understood every word we were saying. Instead of being black, his nose was the pink color of an eraser. His ears, more like a shepherd's than a Lab's, stood at attention.

"In Florida," Luis answered. "They flew to Fort Lauderdale Thursday night. But they're coming back today. I believe there is some party."

"At the Simmons'," I said. "Everyone's invited. You're coming, aren't you?" I hoped I didn't sound too hopeful.

"I wasn't planning to, but now maybe I will." He smiled again.

I smiled back. If I didn't eat all day, I might could get into my black velvet jeans.

"That's it?" Mam said, having finished her interrogation. "You didn't ask him about Hillcrest and what Kit and Miller plan to do? He lives out there."

"I thought Hillcrest was just ruins."

"It is. He's in the old caretaker's house, where you turn off the road by the tomato fields."

"I haven't been out there in years." I tried to visualize the west side of the island. "Is it before Palmetto Point?"

" 'Bout a mile. You should see some of those houses out at Palmetto. That's where Kit and Miller are now. There's enough white columns out there for your Tara World. And a lot of them are just weekend houses for people from Charleston. I don't get it. It's only tidal creek and marsh. If I couldn't be on deep water for the boat, I'd rather be at the beach."

"All the lots are sold. If you want beachfront, you have to buy something that's already there." I pointed at the paper. "And thank goodness we have zoning laws like Edisto, or we'd have high-rises and condos and those Palm Beach-on-steroids houses."

"Amen to that." She stood up. "I need to soak the black-eyed peas for the Hoppin' John for tomorrow. You can wash the collards."

"Gee, thanks," I said. "I don't even really like collards. I'd rather have turnip greens." I looked at her hopefully.

"Nope, fresh collards," she said. "These don't look too sandy. They came from the Caldwells' farm."

"I thought they just did tomatoes."

"No, Miller has him a year-round operation truck farming, here and in Florida. Leastways, that's how I understand it. You know, cold-weather crops—cabbage, collards."

Chloe, who had been doing her impression of a stuffed animal, suddenly lifted her head and barked.

"Hey, I'm back." Bonnie shut the kitchen door behind her. She was wearing the red trouser suit. "Hush, Chloe. It's me, you silly dog." She set her briefcase on the table. "We're finished. The timber company has agreed to settle with the homeowners. There's no bringing back those trees where they clear-cut, but they're going to turn the land into a baseball field and a park. Chalk one up for the good guys."

"Congrats," I said. "The homeowners were smart to fly you down."

"Timing is everything," Bonnie said. "The timber-company president will get to spend New Year's in Jamaica with his third wife, who doesn't look much older than Cissy, and him near old as Daddy and looking like a lizard to boot. Little beady eyes." She shook her head. "Anyway, we lawyers will do the mop-up on Wednesday, and I can fly home Thursday. Plus, I'm back here in time for lunch. What are we having? I'm starving."

Like we'd never heard that before.

"Grilled cheese?" Mam offered. "The tomatoes are terrible this time of year or we could have BLTs."

We often kidded Bonnie that the only reason she'd married Tom was so her initials spelled out her favorite food.

"Grilled cheese is fine," she said. "I'm going to get changed and check on Tom and the boys."

Her voice floated down the stairs a minute later. "Make mine on that wheat bread."

"I'll do it," I volunteered.

"No," Mam said. "I will. You start on those collards."

Darn.

"Where do I turn?" I asked.

"Up there on the left, where that gray truck is pulling out."

We were on the main road heading off the island, on our way to explore what was left of Hillcrest.

"We have to get this mystery solved before I go home," Bonnie had said after polishing off her grilled cheese, the last of Mam's congealed salad, and half a bag of potato chips. "We know Kit was at Pinckney that day before they flew to Florida." She paused long enough to down some iced tea. "And we know Bradford was advising her about restoring Hillcrest. And we know she's not back yet. So now would be a perfect time for us to go out there and see what's left, and if there are any clues."

"I don't know what you think you're going to find out there but a bunch of old bricks," Mam said.

"Maybe a brick was the murder weapon."

"Right," I said. "And Kit just happened to have it in her purse so she could whip it out at the opportune moment and hit Bradford over the head."

"Maybe she just used her purse. Blunt force trauma."

"But why? He was helping her and Miller. They were friends."

"Actually," Mam interjected, "we don't know that for sure. Luis Rivera told you that, Lindsey, but maybe they had a falling-out. The Caldwells didn't come back for the funeral, after all. But they are coming back for the Simmons' party. That's kind of incriminating."

Mam could win a gold medal in the broad jump to conclusions. But I was all for going to Hillcrest, if it meant not washing those collards again. They were still sandy after two rinsings.

I made the turn onto Palmetto Point Road. It was paved but narrow, with ragged shoulders where the asphalt had broken off.

"The tomato trucks sure have torn up this road," Mam said after a particularly vicious bump.

We passed thick stands of pines, palmettos, and water oaks, their leaves still green, mixed in with the bare browns of what I suspected were dogwoods, maples, and crape myrtles. An occasional mailbox indicated a turnoff to someone's drive. Some led to trailers, others to weathered gray houses with sagging, rust-stained tin roofs. One looked abandoned, the kudzu taking over. The thick vines trailed over the porch rails and poked into an open window. I wondered if they had carpeted the floor inside.

"That's Marietta's nephew's place," Mam said, waving at a sandy loam drive lined with the crescents of half-buried whitewall tires.

"He bought that old beach house from the Hendersons and moved it out here, put in a septic tank. His land backs up on the Caldwells'. Slow down. The turn to Hillcrest is coming up on the left after this next curve."

This road wasn't paved. The dirt was packed solid, though, and I tried to stay in the ruts as we jounced past the white cottage where Mam said Luis lived. No car or truck was in sight. And no gold dog.

The tomato fields, plowed under after the last harvest, stretched on either side. Too bad there wasn't a market for weeds. It appeared Miller must have his truck farm on some of his other acreage. Way off to the left was a row of single-story concrete-block buildings, dormitory-style housing for the migrant workers.

"Oh, I keep forgetting," I said. "I thought up a song for us in church yesterday."

"Lindsey, you heathen," Bonnie said. "You were supposed to be listening to the preacher. Bet you can't even remember the sermon."

"Yes, I can. It was on the three wise men. And afterwards, we sang 'We Three Kings,' and that's when I started making up the song."

"Which you are now going to force us to listen to," Mam said, "even though you can't carry a tune in a bucket."

"That's right. Here goes." My singing was as bad as Mam remembered.

We three snoops of Indigo are,
Traveling the island near and far,
Look for mysteries, dig up histories,

Next time, Mam, let's take your car.

I bumped to a stop in front of a gate across the road.

"You just made up that last line," Mam said.

"I know. I was working on something with clues and a star, but this just seemed more appropriate."

"I like it," Bonnie said. "Let's hear the rest."

"There is no rest yet. We can work on it later. So, what do we do now? That's a pretty big lock on that gate, and the barbed-wire fence looks new."

"That's also a very emphatic No Trespassing sign," added Bonnie. "And two Keep Outs."

"Oh, you can buy those at the building supply." Mam had already opened her door. "It's just to discourage hunters and strangers. It doesn't mean us. Just lock the car, and we'll climb over the gate. Hillcrest—or what's left of it—is right up that slope."

"I guess that's why it's called Hillcrest," I said.

I clambered over the gate rails, glad for my tennis shoes. It was just an ordinary farm gate, but I imagined that an elaborate wrought-iron one had greeted long-ago guests to the plantation.

"If it was still standing, it would be one of the oldest manor houses in the country," I said, dredging up memories of Aunt Cora's and Nanny's stories of the island's early days. "It was built before the Revolutionary War and was one of the few brick houses in the area."

"It's probably because it was brick that it lasted as long as it did," Bonnie said. "When was the fire?"

"Not till the 1920s," Mam said. "One of the old Chisholm aunts died in it. She was living out here by herself. Her grave's in the cemetery at the Presbyterian church."

We gazed in silence at the vine-covered ruins, impressive even in decay. Two crumbling chimneys reached toward the sky. The roof was long gone, of course, and one wall had collapsed, but the graceful symmetry of the original structure was still obvious in the arched doorway framed by rectangular windows.

"I wouldn't want to live out here alone," Bonnie said. "It's creepy even in the daytime. Imagine being out here at night." She hunched her shoulders and shivered, then turned back toward the gate. "Uh-oh. We've got company."

A faded gray truck had pulled up next to the CR-V. A stocky man in hunting camouflage and boots stood beside the truck. A black baseball cap shaded his fleshy face, and sunglasses hid his eyes. But he made no effort to hide the shotgun cradled in his arms.

"Come on, y'all." Mam started purposefully for the gate. "Hey, there! Are you with the Caldwells? We're friends of Kit and Miller." That was stretching the truth, but we did know them. "Came out to look at the old house."

The man didn't say anything.

"This'll be a real showpiece when it's fixed up, don't you think?" Mam said. "You were just saying that, weren't you, Bonnie?"

Bonnie nodded vigorously, her blonde hair gleaming in the afternoon sun. "Oh, yes, I was just saying that, wasn't I, Lindsey?"

"Yes, a real showpiece." I couldn't take my eyes off the gun. The light glinted off it, too.

The man suddenly turned to spit a wad of tobacco in the weeds. "Git out."

"There's no need to be so huffy." Mam squared her shoulders. "I told you, we know the owners."

"I said git."

We got.

Bonnie was hoisting herself over the top rail when she stopped. Eye-level with Gun Guy, she peered at him with a puzzled look. "Eddie? Eddie Smoak! It's me, Bonnie Mikell." Her Southern accent was so syrupy we could have used it on pancakes. "Bonnie Tyler now. I live up in D.C. Haven't seen you since high school. Don't you remember me? Bonnie Lynn?"

"I know who you are. Don't make no difference. I ain't one for reunions." He gestured with the gun for Bonnie to get in the CR-V. I already had the keys in the ignition.

"Bye, now," Bonnie said. She shut the door. I couldn't believe she was actually batting her eyelashes at Eddie. A regular Southern belle. "Butthead," she muttered as I pulled away.

For once, Mam didn't bristle at the epithet. "I think we're out of gunshot range," she said, looking at the passenger-side mirror. We bumped down the road. " 'Course, I know objects are closer than they appear. At least he's not following us. Do you think he's on drugs?"

"No," Bonnie said. "He's just a stupid redneck bully. He was in high school, and he still is. Did you see all those bumper stickers on his truck? 'Honk if you hunt.' 'I brake for road kill.' Then there was that one with the deer head: 'If it's brown, it's down.' "

"That's definitely not politically correct," I said. "Speaking of which, Miss Bonnie Lynn, what did you think you were doing back there with that Scarlett O'Hara act?"

"A steel magnolia," she said. "Sometimes it works in Washington."

"Well, it sure didn't work with Eddie," Mam said.

"Fiddle dee dee. I must be losing my touch," Bonnie said.

She laughed as I turned onto Palmetto Point Road and stepped on the gas. "I've got a chorus for 'We Three Snoops.' " Unlike me, Bonnie was on-key.

Oh, Eddie Smoak thinks he's a fright.
But he isn't very bright.
We're still leading, still proceeding,
And in the end, we'll get it right!

"That's good," Mam said. "Let's sing the whole thing."

And so we did. The Dixie Chicks had nothing to worry about.

chapter nine

Round About Midnight

"That side of the Smoak family is just plain common," Aunt Cora said. "Now, Eddie's grandmother Dora Hutto was a real sweet Christian woman, but her daughter Marie, bless her heart, didn't have the sense God gave a goose. Everyone told her not to take up with those Smoaks, but she wouldn't listen. Lie down with dogs, get up with fleas."

Actually, I thought comparing dogs and Smoaks was an insult to most canines, but I knew what she meant.

Eddie Smoak wouldn't be at the Simmons' New Year's Eve party. What I'd told Luis Rivera about everybody being invited was only technically true. Although Ray and Sally called it an open house, a number of islanders wouldn't show up. Indigo was divided less by race than by class. Eddie and his gun-totin', tobacco-chewin' crowd kept mostly to themselves on the island's north end. The Smoak men were either stocky like Eddie or little banty roosters. They always looked funny with the Futches, who came in two sizes, wide and wider. Futch women tended to have thick ankles and bad skin. Lots of children were a given. Every once in a while, one of them would graduate from high school and run off to Atlanta or Charlotte, never to be seen again.

"You sure you don't want me to pick you up for the party?" I asked Aunt Cora.

"No, thank you, child. Margaret Ann called me, too, asking me to go with them, but I think I'll just stay right here and watch the TV. I talked to Maudie earlier, and she's doing the same thing. We're going to have us a little New Year's dinner tomorrow out at her place. You young folks go ahead and have a good time."

"You'll miss the Frogmore Stew."

"Humph," Aunt Cora said. "I've eaten plenty of it in my day, and it doesn't set as well as it once did. You can have my share."

I love Frogmore Stew, or Beaufort Boil, as some people call the Low Country specialty. But if I ate even my share of shrimp and crab cooked with chunks of corn on the cob, sausage, and potato, I might bust out of my black jeans.

It looked, though, as if there would be plenty of takers for the feast. Cars, trucks, and SUVs lined both sides of the street. I had to park three houses down.

Despite the cold, a group was gathered around the oysters roasting in the side yard, near where Ray Simmons was laboring over the cookers for the stew. There was probably extra beer in the coolers sitting next to the Jeep under the house, but I could tell from the noise spilling into the night that the main bar was upstairs on the side porch.

"Lindsey, happy New Year, sugar!" Sally Simmons, her red hair contrasting with her spangled emerald shirt over matching velour trousers, directed me toward the front bedroom. Coats covered the king-sized duvet, but I spotted Mam's suede jacket. Good, they were already here.

"Hello, Miss Fox." Olivia Washington was checking her lipstick in the dresser mirror, her back to me.

"It's Lindsey," I said automatically. "I was so glad to hear Marietta's going to be all right. Is there any more news?"

"No," Olivia said curtly, sticking the lipstick in the pocket of her wool coat before taking it off to add to the pile on the bed.

I couldn't understand why she still seemed angry with me. It had become obvious last night that Marietta was run down before I got there. Maybe Olivia didn't like it that her boss was my alibi.

"Oh, Olivia, I love that sweater!" I said.

"Mm," she grunted, her back still to me.

"No, really," I said. "Look." I slipped off my own jacket to reveal the twin to Olivia's gold sweater, only mine was red.

It was the first time I'd seen her smile. It turned her into a whole different person.

"Chico's!" we said in unison.

"I really love their clothes," she said. "That red looks good on you."

"And I love that gold," I said. "We are obviously women of taste and style."

"I can hardly wait for that January sale," she said.

Apparently, the sweaters dispelled whatever doubts she had about me. I let her lead us through the throng in the dining room and out to the side porch. She was so tall that I felt like a dinghy behind a yacht, but that was okay. We had bonded.

"You want a beer?" I said. My bottle of Michelob was wet with ice from the cooler.

"No, I'm on duty starting at ten," she said. "Will—I mean Major McLeod—is working all night, but he told me to come to the party till then."

It was a good thing Ray and Sally had such a big house. Their party had become a tradition in just the four years since he'd built on one of the few deepwater lots on Indigo's marshy west side. The house, which had been photographed for *Southern Interiors*, had all the extras, including tiled porches that converted from glass to screens according to the season, cathedral ceilings, oak cabinets, and a two-sided fireplace dividing the kitchen and living room.

There were a few faces I didn't recognize—probably newcomers or friends of Ray and Sally's from Charleston. I saw the Padgetts, who were friends of my parents, nodding at something Beth Chesnut was saying. I wondered if she was going to angle again for Bradford's job. I'd have to ask Mam.

"Hello, foxy lady." Jamie Townsend appeared beside me at the buffet, drink in hand. He obviously didn't know how often I heard that—and how much I hated it. "You look positively gorgeous," he said, moving closer, "and you smell heavenly. You can run over me any day. Just don't run away."

I backed off from his bourbon breath. "And me without my Nikes. I'll just have to do the best I can."

"Oh, you can run, but you won't be able to hide forever."

Jamie obviously thought he was a hottie. Granted, he was good looking, but conceit and Jack Daniel's had combined to make him a legend in his own mind. Even now, he was scanning the crowd for another possible conquest.

I grabbed some cheese straws and made a beeline to where Mam and Bonnie were standing with their backs to me, talking to someone in a wing chair by the fireplace.

"Oh, Lindsey," Mam gushed. "Let me introduce you to Penelope Upchurch."

"Oh, please just call me Pen." She was all in black, her sleek blonde hair pulled back from her face with an ebony velvet bow.

"Well, nicknames work for us," I said.

"Oh, I know. Margaret Ann and Bonnie were just explaining the Mam and BLT names to me. I think that is just adorable. And their mama is Boodie. Now, I had an aunt who was a Lady. That was her name, I mean. Lady Upchurch."

"Mm," I said. "Sounds like royalty. There's not really a short way to say Lindsey, although I still get called Fox by friends from college."

"Oh, Bradford never wanted anyone to call him Brad. It had to be Bradford. But it suited him somehow. He was very detail oriented and liked everything just so."

"I'm very sorry about your loss," I said. I hoped I sounded sincere. It was the standard opening I'd had to use when I was a reporter interviewing people right after a tragedy. It was followed by the question I always hated asking: How do you feel? Like I didn't already know from the stricken looks or tear-stained cheeks.

"Oh, it was a shock." Pen's face was sober, her voice soft. "I still can't quite take it in. I think I must be on automatic pilot. Even though we were divorced, we stayed in touch."

"And it's such a small world." Mam, wearing the new blue sweater J. T. had given her for Christmas, looked pleased as punch. Her face was flushed, meaning she'd also been enjoying Sally's champagne punch. "Pen just told us, Lindsey, that she and Kit Caldwell were sorority sisters. She's been down here staying with them, and she's going to help Kit buy the antiques to refurnish Hillcrest when the time comes. I told her we just rode out there this afternoon."

"I've already started doing the research," Pen said. "Because Hillcrest was a colonial-era house, rather than an antebellum one like Pinckney, I expect I'll be able to find more things in Philadelphia than in Charleston. Bradford and I were talking about that just last Tuesday when I met him for lunch at the Charleston Grill."

"I love their marinated fillet," Mam said.

Count on the conversation to turn to food. Now, here she was suggesting that maybe the four of us and Kit could all get together for lunch later in the week, before Bonnie had to fly home to Washington and Pen to Philadelphia.

"Oh, that would be so nice," Pen said. "I'm here until Friday. You know, I wouldn't be at this party—I didn't think it looked right—but Kit insisted I come with her and Miller. I wanted to go stay at a hotel in Charleston when they had to rush off to Florida, but Kit wouldn't hear of it. And really, that turned out to be a blessing in a way, with what happened." Her face started to crumple. "You girls excuse me. I'm going to find the powder room."

She quickly slipped through the crowd, keeping her head down.

"Oh, the poor thing," Mam said. "She's still right cut-up about Bradford. Maybe she was still in love with him. Makes you wonder how long they'd been divorced."

"She was obviously too good for him," Bonnie said. "Don't

you think that with that cute little figure and blonde hair, she looks a little bit like Will's Darlene?"

"She's hardly Will's Darlene anymore," I reminded them, trying to contain any cattiness in my voice. It certainly wasn't Pen's fault that she looked like Darlene. But I did wonder what her real hair color was.

"Speaking of Will, where is he?" Mam asked, looking around. "Have you talked to him any more about that bone?"

"What's this about a bone?" asked our host, suddenly appearing with a drink in each hand.

Thanks to a nose like a blade and a silver widow's peak, Ray looked like a bird of prey. He certainly had an eye for development opportunities. Where others saw marsh grass and mud flats, Ray colored in condos and putting greens. Until the Magnolia Cay project, though, he had built only a couple of spec houses on Indigo, instead working his deals over at Kiawah and up near Myrtle Beach.

"Oh, Ray, this is such a nice party," Mam said. "You and Sally have outdone yourselves this year."

"Glad you're having a good time, but pretty ladies shouldn't be standing around talking about bones."

"Oh, it's just this big bone Jimmy McLeod found out at Pinckney," Mam said.

I could have kicked her, but Ray was in the way.

"Probably a deer," Ray said. "There used to be a couple good stands back there when Pinck and I were teenagers."

Bonnie and I nodded.

"I suspect so," I said.

"No, you don't," Mam said, even though Bonnie and I were giving her the hairy eyeball. "And neither does Will McLeod.

Otherwise, he wouldn't have taken it to the lab for testing."

"Just a precaution, I'm sure," Ray said. "Those woods are full of deer this year. What I came to tell you girls is that we're bringing up the stew. Sally says for everybody to get their plates and dig in. Let me go round up that group by the TV."

As soon as he was out of earshot, Bonnie turned on Mam. "Why on earth did you tell him about the bone? Ray, of all people. And you told Pen we were out at Hillcrest, and you know she'll tell Kit. And since when did you want to start having lunch with Kit Caldwell, anyway? I thought you didn't like her."

"I don't," Mam said. "But I like Pen, and I thought maybe if we have lunch with her and Kit, we'll find out something." Her voice rose defensively. "Don't you think that's a good idea, Lindsey?"

"Maybe." We were slowly working our way to the dining room. "But let's not talk about it here." I waved J. T. over. "Here, take my place. I'm going to get a Coke."

That was true. But I also had spotted a dark head out on the porch.

"You came," I said. Oh, brilliant observation.

"Yes." Luis Rivera smiled. "I came."

"But no dog." My conversational abilities had suddenly deserted me. It wasn't like I didn't know good-looking guys, but there was something about the way Luis looked at me with those bedroom eyes.

"No, no dog."

Before I could say anything else and make a further fool of myself, I felt a large hand on my shoulder.

"It's Lindsey, right?" Miller Caldwell beamed down at me. "Saw you last summer at the fire-department fish fry. You're the magazine writer. And I see you've met Luis. Good man, Luis. He's my right hand. Couldn't do without him."

It was almost impossible not to smile at Miller. A big teddy bear of a man with a ruddy face, he exuded goodwill. Too bad he was stuck with Kit, who could frost you with one glance. That is, if she even bothered to acknowledge you. Most of the time, she was too busy looking over your shoulder to see if there was someone more important she could talk to.

"Hey, Miller. I haven't seen Kit yet."

He looked around vaguely. "She's here somewhere. She may be with Pen. I don't know if you've met her yet or not, but she was married to Bradford Bentley." He shook his head. "Can you believe it, falling down the stairs like that and dying? They say falls are one of the leading causes of accidental death, but I always thought they were talking about old people. Never expect it to happen to someone your age, that's for sure. It makes you think, it really does." His double chin jiggled. "Here, let's drink a little toast to Bradford."

He tapped his glass to my and Luis's beer bottles. I realized Miller was well on his way to being drunk.

"To my friend Bradford," he said.

"To Bradford," I said weakly.

"Bradford," echoed Luis.

"Oh, darling, here you are." Kit loomed next to Miller. "And here's Luis. And I don't believe we've had the pleasure."

Geez Louise. She knew perfectly well who I was.

"Lindsey Fox," I reminded her. "Cora Hudson's my great-aunt." Might as well bring out the big guns.

"Oh, of course." Kit looked at me appraisingly. I was pleased to see that she had the beginnings of a zit on her aristocratic nose. "You've done something different with your hair. Very nice."

"Thank you." I'd worn some version of a pageboy the last ten years.

Kit turned away from me. "Miller, dear, there are some friends of Ray's I want you to meet. From Charleston."

He followed her like a St. Bernard trailing a whippet. I had dogs on the brain.

"You want another beer?" Luis was fishing in the cooler.

"A Coke, please."

I took too quick a gulp and felt the liquid dribble down my chin. Another brilliant move. Then again, it might be.

"Allow me." Luis dabbed my face with his handkerchief. If he were a woman, Maybelline would have signed him on the spot for those eyelashes.

"Sorry to interrupt, Lindsey."

Will had come out of nowhere. He was wearing his uniform, cap in hand.

"Luis, I need to speak with you a minute. Lindsey, if you'll excuse us, please."

"Sure." I walked away, wondering what that was about.

I saw Olivia by the kitchen door. She had her coat on. Surely, it wasn't ten yet.

"Bye, Lindsey. Have a happy New Year."

"You're leaving already?"

"Yes. We got a report of shots fired out on Palmetto Point Road near Hillcrest. Probably just fireworks going off early. I'll need to stay and cover the beach."

"Be careful," I said as she went out the door.

"Excuse us, Lindsey." Will brushed past me with Luis. They must be going to Hillcrest, too.

"Yes, sir." I saluted and moved out of the way.

Will appeared not to notice. Luis looked serious but then smiled. "Happy New Year, Lindsey Fox."

"Happy New Year."

I sighed. There went any chance of a New Year's Eve kiss. I might as well go stuff myself with stew. My sweater would cover the top of my jeans when I unbuttoned them.

Someone had turned up the stereo, and couples were starting to shag to "Sixty Minute Man." J. T., who was singing under his breath, had a drink in one hand and Mam by the other.

Jamie, his face flushed, stretched out his arm to me. "C'mon, Lindsey," he said. "Let's show 'em how it's really done. I took shag lessons last year."

Oh, great. A beginner. Those of us who had grown up with beach music couldn't quite get over the younger crowd, who thought they'd invented the dance. 'Course, they were better than the Yankees who confused shagging with Austin Powers movies.

Jamie wasn't bad, but I sure hoped he hadn't had any swing lessons. My stomach wouldn't be able to take it. I saw Bonnie at the dessert table, homing in on the cakes. Pound, caramel, red velvet, rum. She'd be there all night.

Jamie swung me close and breathed heavily in my ear. I nimbly sidestepped him as the song ended and he attempted a dip. As much as he'd been drinking, he'd probably drop me.

"What say we ditch this crowd and go for a little ride?" he slurred. "You know, I'm working with Dad and Ray on Magnolia Cay, and I can show you where we're going to put the community dock."

"I'll take a rain check," I said. As curious as I was about the development, I wasn't about to get in a car with a drunk.

"Speaking of checks, I need to go check on Bonnie before she ODs on rum cake."

Jamie didn't seem offended. But he looked a little green around the gills at the mention of rum cake.

I decided to wait to tell the others about the possible shots near Hillcrest. Knowing Mam, she'd have to be restrained from getting in the car and going to see firsthand. At the very least, she'd want to call Will, and I didn't want Olivia to regret having told me something she probably shouldn't have.

Luis didn't come back to the party, but that was to be expected, especially after I saw Miller on his cell phone. He, Kit, and Pen left shortly thereafter. Pen, apparently the designated driver, waved good-bye with her car keys.

"I don't think she's really in a party mood," Mam said. "Maybe we could see her without Kit. Did you know that woman acted like she never met Bonnie before?"

"She pulled the same trick with me." I peeled a shrimp, then looked at Mam's plate. "You have any cocktail sauce left? Kit's either so spaced-out that she really does draw a blank, or else she's a really good actress."

"If she's such a good actress, Miss Augusta ought to sign her up for the next Indigo Players production," Bonnie said. She picked at a few cake crumbs on her plate.

In addition to running Pinckney, Miss Augusta headed up the local community theater. As she'd told us on more than one occasion, she had been the leading light of the Fort Bragg Playhouse when she and Carter were stationed in North Carolina. Now, she usually directed the seasonal productions, but islanders were still talking about her star turn several years back in *Everybody Loves Opal*.

Like Aunt Cora, Miss Augusta had elected to miss Ray and Sally's party. Pinck had told us she was staying in Charleston through New Year's Day. More shrimp for the rest of us.

I drove home shortly after midnight. Considering my track record with New Year's Eves, this one had been better than most. Last year at this time, I was still seeing Mark Wright, but he'd been covering the Sugar Bowl. Sports columnists are rarely around on weekends and holidays. I usually was at Indigo on New Year's anyway. At least we now had Ray and Sally's to go to. Better than staying home and watching *Gone With the Wind* with Mam, which was what we did once when J. T. had the flu.

Bonnie and I had hugged at midnight, and J. T. had given us each a quick peck after planting a big kiss on Mam. Then Bonnie had taken her cell phone up to the second-floor porch to see if she could reach Tom. I said good-bye to Sally, who was telling her son, Skeet, that on no account could he set off bottle rockets from the roof: "Remember the drought, sugar. You're liable to burn down the island."

As I turned on the beach road, I saw Olivia's cruiser parked at Cap's filling station. I flicked my lights in greeting and was surprised when she pulled out to follow me.

"It was nice of you to see me home," I said, walking down the driveway.

"Wanted to make sure you were safe and sound."

"Oh, Will, I thought you were Olivia. She said something about being down here, and I really didn't expect to see you. Everything all right?"

"Everything's fine," he said. "It's been a fairly quiet night. We thought there might be some trouble out at the Caldwells', but it was just Eddie Smoak showing off his new shotgun. Here, I'll walk you to your door."

"You don't have to do that."

He was already out of the car. "I want to."

He followed me up the stairs. I put the key in the door, then turned to say good night.

"Happy New Year, Lindsey."

"Happy—"

Will's lips stopped mine. I had my New Year's Eve kiss after all.

chapter ten

Bonnie's a Butterbean, or Aunt Cora with the Candlestick

"I'm a boiled peanut."

"What?" I asked.

"I'm a boiled peanut," Mam repeated. "That means you are, too."

"What on earth are you talking about?" I moaned sleepily. "And why are you calling me at"—I cocked one eye at the bedside clock—"eight in the morning on New Year's Day?"

"Our mothers always call each other at eight."

This was true. They'd been doing it for years, except for the times when one called the other earlier to say she couldn't call at eight.

"I've been calling you at the same time every morning," Mam said. "You haven't complained before."

"I was awake before," I said. "Stop, Peaches." He was patting me on the face with his paw to let me know he was awake, too.

Just so I got the message, he began chewing on my hair. "I'll feed you in a minute. Now, what's this about boiled peanuts?" I untangled myself from the cat and sat up in bed.

"It's this Southern horoscope thing that's going round the Internet. Ashley e-mailed it to Cissy. She's upset because she's a crawfish, and according to this, crawfish tend not to be physically attractive. And they're not, except I guess to other crawfish, or maybe a lobster. Crawfish look like little lobsters."

She'd gotten me up to explain the dating habits of shellfish?

"But you and I are both boiled peanuts, and J. T. is grits. And I think that's exactly right, because you don't eat boiled peanuts and grits together in the morning, and I'm a morning person, but it always takes J. T. at least two cups of coffee to get going. But later in the day, boiled peanuts and grits are good together, and so are J. T. and I." She sounded pleased with this observation.

All this talk of food was making me slightly queasy. "Mam—"

"Bonnie's a butterbean. Don't you think that fits? Oh, I forgot you haven't seen the list. You can read it when you come over. It's real cute. But that's not the reason I called."

"It isn't?"

"No, I need you to do me a favor."

Anything, I thought, if she would leave off talking about butterbeans and crawfish.

"Look in your mama's spice rack and see if she's got some Goya ham seasoning. I thought I had a ham bone in the freezer, but when I went to get it this morning, I remembered I used it to make split pea soup. I need the seasoning to cook the collards."

Collards. Ye gods.

"Hoppin' John for luck, collards for money," said J. T., pushing back from the table. "Can't ask for more than that on New Year's Day. Except maybe some dessert."

"You're on your own for that," Mam said. "There's pecan pie on the counter, and I made sweet potato pie, too. But I don't want any now. Soon as us girls get the dishes in the dishwasher, we're going over to the beach and walk off some of these holiday calories."

The weather had warmed up considerably, yet supposedly another cold front was on the way. Meantime, I didn't even need a jacket over my turtleneck.

"Can I come with y'all?" Cissy asked. "Jimmy's hunting all day, and Daddy's just going to fall asleep watching football."

"The more the merrier," I said. "I'll drive."

"Before we go to the beach, Aunt Lindsey, could we run by Pinckney? I forgot to get my paycheck Thursday, and I really need to put it in the bank tomorrow. I've got a key to the back door, and I know the entry code to the gate, if Miss Augusta's not there."

I didn't tell her I knew the entry code, too, although I'd told Bonnie and Mam I'd figured out Julia's age from the cemetery.

"It's high tide, so there's no beach to walk on yet. We might as well go to Pinckney first," Mam said. "And it's a pretty day for a drive."

It was exactly that, the sky a clear, cloudless blue and not another car on the road. We passed the Murray place, a two-story white frame house where there must have been a dozen cars and trucks.

"That's Carrie's new Mustang," Cissy said. "Her daddy said if she made the honor roll, he'd get her a car for Christmas. I made the honor roll, and I didn't get a car."

"We don't pay for grades," Mam said. "You know that. If you keep saving that paycheck of yours, you'll have enough money for a car one day."

"By that time, I'll be in college, and freshmen can't have cars."

"I know," Mam said, not without some satisfaction.

"Mom . . ."

Cissy was play-pouting. This was hardly the first time they'd had this conversation, and I knew it wouldn't be the last. And one of these days, Mam was going to get tired of either handing Cissy her car keys or hauling her out to Pinckney.

I let Cissy punch us in the gate. The avenue of live oaks with arching, moss-dripping limbs might look like a cliché, but it was still breathtaking. It was peaceful, too, without cars full of visitors or busloads of Germans on plantation package tours. Cissy said that they covered Natchez to Charleston in two weeks. It was a far cry from horse-and-carriage days, when Pinckney was in its prime.

"Well, Miss Augusta's not here," Cissy said. "It's so spooky going in the house when it's empty, especially with all that's happened."

"Sometimes, I think it really is haunted," Mam said. "We sure heard enough strange noises when we worked here."

"Things that went bump in the night," I said. "Only sometimes, it was broad daylight, like now."

"Oh, every old house has creaks and groans," Bonnie said. "I never can understand why people say houses are still. They may not be getting up and walking around, but things don't stay still. I'd love to get a chance to really look around this place while Miss Augusta's not here. After all, I wasn't on the scene with y'all last week."

I pulled up the back drive. "Well, I'm not going anywhere near the third floor," I said. "Look at what happened the last time we went snooping."

"Well, at least let me peek in the cellar," Bonnie said.

"You can say hello to the snakes and the spiders for me," I said.

"It's winter," Mam said. "The snakes are all hibernating."

"Right," I said. "Hibernating underneath Miss Augusta's house. If you go down there, don't go picking up any rope." Like other island houses, Pinckney was built up off the ground, but part of the latticed area below the first floor had been enclosed to form a small basement. I seriously doubted it was rodent- and reptile-proof.

"You haven't seen the Christmas decorations, Aunt Bonnie," Cissy said. She unlocked the back door. "Let me get my check out of the office, and I'll show you the parlor. It's been repainted a real pretty St. Cecilia blue. Isn't that neat? That's there's blue named for me?"

"Named for St. Cecilia," Mam said, opening the door of the refrigerator.

Typical. "Exactly what are you expecting to find in there?" I asked. "The ghost of Christmas past?"

"More like milk past its sell-by date," Mam said. "I'm going to go ahead and clear out this old stuff, so Miss Augusta won't have to worry with it when she gets back. I don't know how she's going to get along without Marietta."

I left her searching for garbage bags under the sink and wandered out to the foyer. The petticoat table—so named because of its low, built-in mirror, in which ladies checked the hems of their crinolines—already had a layer of fine dust on it. I swirled my finger through it. *LLF*. Then I drew a heart. And a *W*.

Stop it, I told myself. I was acting like a love-struck teen. I stuck out my tongue at myself in the hall mirror. A shadow flickered in one corner, and I turned to look up the stairs behind me. Nothing there. Must have been my imagination.

My eyes followed the fruit garland up the mahogany rail of the cantilevered staircase, which appeared to float in the air. The afternoon sun streamed in the landing window, and dust motes danced in the light.

"Hey, Bonnie, Cissy, are y'all up there?"

No answer.

I started up the stairs but froze on the third step. I was sure I'd heard a creak, as if someone had stepped on one of the stairs above me I couldn't see. Maybe Mam had gone up the back stairs from the kitchen.

"Mam?" I called.

"What?" she said, coming up behind me.

"Geez, you scared me!" I said, steadying myself on the railing. "I thought I heard something up there."

"Not a thud, was it?"

"No, more of a creak. And before that, there was a flicker in the mirror."

"That was probably a branch scraping the window. See? Bonnie was right. Old houses aren't quiet, whether they're haunted or not. You're just imagining stuff."

But Mam didn't sound as brave as her words. She always acted in charge, but she could get as spooked as me. Neither of us liked scary stuff. We'd gone together to see the first *Halloween* movie and ended up cramming ourselves in one seat, watching with our hands in front of our faces. And when we were little, she always had to sleep with a sheet on her, even in the hottest of weather, because she thought it would protect her from the crazed killer with a knife she was sure was going to cut through the screen door one night.

That was Daddy and Uncle James's fault. They'd gotten a kick out of telling us ghost stories, terrorizing us with tales of headless horsemen and the phantom who kept intoning, "Give me back my golden arm." Worst of all were the stories of a certain Ronnie Rondoli, who roamed Indigo living off rats and raccoons, chickens if he could get them. But what he liked best of all, Uncle James told us in a hushed tone, was small children.

"Remember Ronnie Rondoli?" I asked. "We used to hear him scratching on Nanny's screen porch when we were sleeping out there."

"That was just our daddies trying to scare us," Mam said. "They did a pretty good job, too. Didn't Bonnie wet the bed? Or was it Jack?"

"They each claimed it was the other," I said. "I think that was the last time they slept together, though. We had to take Bonnie in with us after that. And she snored."

"She still does," Mam said, giggling. "Come on and let's go. I already took the trash out. Bonnie and Cissy are in the kitchen. Bonnie took one look down the cellar stairs and thought a walk on the beach was a lot more appealing."

"What's that you're holding?"

"Oh, just some historical-society stuff that Cissy saw on the desk in the office," Mam said. She hefted a large cardboard box under one arm and brushed some dust off her red corduroy jeans. "I think it's Aunt Cora's, because this is her handwriting on the top here. She must have brought it over and forgot it. Looks like minutes from some of the meetings. She's secretary, I think, or archivist. There are some old photos in here, too. I thought we could swing by her house on the way to the beach and drop them off."

Cissy locked the back door and jiggled it to make sure it was shut tight. "What's this doing here?" she said, leaning over to pick up a big white conch shell from beneath the azalea by the back steps. "Miss Augusta uses it as a doorstop. It's, like, one of the biggest ones ever found on Indigo."

"Oh, I remember it," I said. "Some great-great-uncle who went and got killed in the Civil War found it out at the inlet when he was a boy."

"I wonder what it's doing out here," Cissy said.

"Who knows?" Mam said. "But bring it with you and we'll give it to Miss Augusta later, since it's an heirloom. Just looks like another big whelk you'd find after a storm. Uncle Lee still has his, doesn't he, Lindsey?"

"Yes. He used it for an ashtray before he quit smoking."

A small black car rounded the side of the house. Beth Chesnut looked as surprised to see us as we were to see her.

"Why, Happy New Year, Beth," Mam said. "We just ran by so Cissy could get her paycheck."

"Happy New Year," Beth said, nodding at us.

She looked like she hadn't recovered from last night's party. There were dark circles under her eyes, and the sunshine highlighted lines around her mouth and nose. Like us, she hadn't bothered with makeup today. Unlike us, she needed it. But maybe I was too critical. And maybe I was a little jealous because she and Mam were such good friends and I was left out. I wondered if Bonnie felt the same way.

"I had to leave early last Thursday," Beth said. "You know, before everything happened." She fluttered her hands. "And I realized this afternoon that I'd left the December inventory sheets for the gift shop. Even though we're closed for January, I need to start getting orders in for the spring. You know, we're down to about our last tote bag, and we sold completely out of the Indigo note cards. That company does such a nice job. I was thinking about having them do the invitations for Sue Beth's wedding."

Lord, Beth could talk even more than Mam. No wonder the two of them were tight as ticks.

"You know, Beth," Mam said, "I bet we could talk Miss Augusta into letting you have the reception here at Pinckney now. I never did understand why Bradford was so dead set on not having any private parties here this spring. That landscaping always seemed like a sorry excuse."

"Oh, do you really think Miss Augusta might agree?" Beth said. "Y'know, this is horrible"—she lowered her voice—"but when I first heard about Bradford, I thought, well, at least now I wouldn't have to invite him to the wedding. We really are trying to keep it kind of small, but with me being so involved with the historical society, I knew I had to put him on the guest list. I tell you, planning a wedding takes a lot of time and energy. You just wait till it's Cissy's turn."

I opened the car door. If we didn't get out of here soon, Beth and Mam would start talking bridesmaids' dresses and caterers. Bonnie was already in the front seat. We looked at each other, and Bonnie nodded. Maybe she was a little tired of Mam's Beth-this and Beth-that, too.

I honked the horn, and Mam and Beth jumped. Bonnie grinned.

"Geez, guess we just got crossed off the guest list."

"Aunt Cora's not here," I said, parking in front of her house. "At least her car's not in the driveway. She must still be at Miss Maudie's. You want to leave that stuff on the porch?" I turned in the seat and looked at Mam. "Or do you want to give it to Miss Rachel?"

"Heavens, no," Mam said. "She'd be interrogating us. We'll take it home and give it to her tomorrow. But here, Cissy, let me write Cora a note that we were here, and you can stick it in the mailbox."

"You know Miss Rachel will tell her," I said, watching Cissy deposit the note.

"All the more reason for us to leave her a note, so she'll be one up when Rachel calls. What is Cissy doing?"

Having stopped to straighten the wreath on Cora's door and tweak its red bow, Cissy was now peering in the glass.

"Cissy, come on!" Mam hollered out the window.

"What were you looking at?" she asked a minute later as Cissy tugged her seatbelt on.

"It was on the hall table," Cissy said. "I saw something winking in the sun, and I wanted to see what it was." She stopped. "A big silver candlestick. Like the one that's been missing from Pinckney."

chapter eleven

Home Matters

"Haven't I seen these candlesticks before?" I asked, holding one of the tall pair from Margaret Ann's dining-room table up to the light from the window.

She'd given me a choice when I'd walked in the door this morning. Either I could pick out pecans—"You can watch the video of Cissy cheerleading while you do that"—or I could put away the silver in the dining room while she packed up the Dickens Village. Seeing as how she'd offered to wash my clothes with hers, I handed over the laundry bag in exchange for the silver chest.

"Of course you've seen them before," she said, matching the socks she'd just taken from the dryer. "They were Nanny's."

"How did you wrest them away from our mothers?"

"Oh, Nanny gave them to me before she died. You know how she was those last few years. If you said you liked something, she'd say you could have it when she was gone. Thought for sure she'd forget. But then when we started going through the house after the funeral, there were those little pieces of masking tape on the bottoms of things. Isn't that how you got the blue-and-white teapot?"

"Yes, and Jack ended up with that tacky black-velvet painting of Niagara Falls that used to be in the front bedroom. Jill made him hang it in the garage."

"You'd be surprised how much some of those old black-velvet paintings are worth," Mam said. "If the computer was working, we could look some up on eBay. It was giving Cissy fits last night, kept freezing up when she was trying to print out something she needed for school today. Naturally, she waited to the last minute. But she was ready before J. T. this morning. Bonnie didn't leave till about eight."

"Why would she?" I said. "She said that meeting wasn't until ten."

"She was going to go by the courthouse in Centerville first, remember? To check on those records on Magnolia Cay."

Bonnie had been intrigued by the glossy brochures Ray and Pinck spread on the coffee table at the New Year's Eve party. "I thought this part of Pinckney Plantation was a conservation easement," she'd said. Seeing our blank looks, she explained that easements generally limited development and preserved open space for wildlife preserves or recreational uses. "It has to do with the Taxpayer Relief Law of 1997. A conservation easement is what saved one of the old plantations on Wadmalaw. But I may be wrong where Pinckney's concerned. Maybe it's just protected wetlands. But either way, it could explain why they're having trouble with permits."

"I forgot," I said. My encounter with Will had erased much of the party from my mind. I'd expected him to call yesterday or last night. I was mad at him for not calling, and mad at myself for caring.

"I think you've polished that candlestick enough," Mam said, giving me a shrewd look.

I admired its gleam. "Why do you really think Aunt Cora has that candlestick from Pinckney at her house?"

"Like I said yesterday, she's probably going to take it to Charleston for resilvering."

"But why just one?"

"Maybe there is just one," Mam said. "I'm going to go check on those whites before I start on the Dickens." Then she called back over her shoulder: "Maybe it's the murder weapon."

"Oh, Lord, Mam," I said. "We know Aunt Cora didn't kill Bradford."

She would have to bring up Bradford. Really, I was doing my level best not to think about anything remotely involving Will. I had woken up this morning—to a phone call from Mam, naturally, asking to borrow Mama's nutcracker—with a firm resolution to put Will and the past behind me. Over the years, I'd thought from time to time about moving back to Indigo, but working in Charlotte at the TV station and then at the newspaper had made that impossible. Even after I left the paper to freelance and then took the job with *Perfect Pet*, there had been other reasons to stay in Charlotte.

Like Mark Wright, who turned out to be Mr. Wrong, although

it took a couple of stormy years to finally admit that when it came to our relationship, I was the only one rowing that boat. I had finally bailed out last summer, although giving up on Mark was one of the hardest things I'd ever had to do. He hadn't broken my heart like Will, but there had been some emotional bruises.

"You know it's for the best," my friend Vaughn had consoled me. "Mark's a good-time guy, but you know he's not one for the long haul."

I'd missed him this fall, though, discovering anew the dearth of available men. "They're all either married or gay," I complained to Vaughn. "Or else they're divorced for a very good reason."

This came after she'd set me up with a business friend of her husband, Alan. What a disaster. The guy had spent our entire dinner telling me what a bitch his ex-wife was, and then didn't understand why I didn't want to continue the conversation at his high-rise condo.

"Who's that in the driveway behind your car?" Mam asked, reappearing with a wicker laundry basket piled high with our "delicates," as Nanny called them.

"It's Pen," I said, looking out the window.

Mam came to stand by me. "Wonder where she's headed all dressed up," she said.

Pen was wearing a gray gabardine trouser suit that I was pretty sure I'd seen at Ann Taylor and flinched at the price tag. Her black shoes were either Kenneth Cole or an expensive knockoff in Italian leather.

"Hey, Pen," Mam said, opening the front door. "What brings you here? Excuse all the mess. We've been doing after-holiday chores. Would you like some coffee or tea, maybe a Coke? Here, come on in the family room and sit down."

"Thanks," Pen said. She smiled, but her eyes were busy appraising Mam's décor. Of course, she was an antiques dealer. "I can't stay long. I should have called from Kit's, but I'm in a bit of a rush. I'm going to Charleston to meet with Henry Colleton and Bradford's lawyer, and then straight on to the airport. You know, I had to delay my return flight after, well, after everything, and it looked like I couldn't get to Philadelphia until Friday. But now I can get a flight tonight. I didn't want to go without saying good-bye, though."

"I should think not," Mam said, settling next to Pen on the overstuffed sage tweed sofa. She motioned me to the club chair. I couldn't resist swinging my blue-jeaned legs over the arm, despite Mam's frown. "Now, what about something to drink? Lindsey will be glad to get it."

But of course.

"No, nothing for me," Pen said. "Is Bonnie not here?"

"No, she'll be so sorry she missed you and we won't have our lunch in Charleston. But she had meetings this morning. I think she wanted to look up those permit requests for Magnolia Cay, too. You know, environmental law is her specialty, and she didn't really realize until New Year's what a big development Ray and Pinck are planning." Mam picked up one of the brochures on the end table. "Bonnie was concerned about all the proposed bulkheads along the marsh front." She pointed to an artist's rendering of a large house and dock that looked like some we'd seen over at Kiawah. "It's hard to get permit approval, because the rules are always changing. She also was going to check the water rights for that whole tract of land, wasn't she, Lindsey?"

I nodded, but before I could say anything, Mam was telling Pen how Bonnie and Tom might want to buy a lot at Magnolia

Cay. "They've always said that when he retires from the military, they'll settle on Indigo."

This might be news to Tom, who'd grown up on Maryland's Eastern Shore. But I knew Bonnie was an island girl at heart. So was I, although I'd gone out of state to college, thanks to my high-school journalism teacher. Her husband, another Tar Heel, was the baseball coach who'd made sure Will got a scholarship at Chapel Hill. But like so many islanders, we hadn't returned after college, because there were so few jobs. If Daddy hadn't been a C.P.A. and Uncle James an architect, both with businesses of their own, we might not have even grown up on Indigo.

"As a matter of fact, Bradford was one of Ray's first investors," Pen said. "He had one of those deepwater lots on Molasses Creek. I suppose Ray gave him a deal if he would build one of the first houses out there. Good for future business, and that sort of thing."

She smoothed her manicured hands in her lap, then rose from the sofa. "Well, that's a moot point now. And speaking of Bradford, that's why we're meeting today. Henry and I are co-executors of his will, it turns out, and Henry's maybe going to try and finish his manuscript on the Pinckneys and island history. Only problem is, I can't seem to locate all Bradford's computer disks. I found several when I was at that condo he was renting. That good-looking deputy—McLeod, is it?—was with me. Still, Bradford must not have done as much as I thought, or else some of his research is missing. Do you think any of the historical-society members would know anything about other disks? Maybe Miss Augusta?"

"I know where two disks are!" Mam exclaimed. "Maybe it's Bradford's writing on the labels." She reached into the box Cissy had put in the hallway after our trip to Pinckney. "They were with some historical-society stuff we picked up yesterday and were going to give to Aunt Cora. Here's one. Can you tell if it's his writing, Pen?"

But before Pen could even look at the disk, Mam changed direction and headed down the hall. "Let me put this in the computer and check for you, just in case it has nothing to do with the manuscript."

"Oh, you don't need to do that," Pen called after her. "There's really not time. I'll have Henry check when I get to Charleston, and if it's not, I'm sure he'll get it to Miss Augusta or your aunt. I'm going to be late meeting him as it is." She turned to me. "Did she say there were two disks?"

I rummaged through the box—old photos, a manila envelope of letters, a membership roster. "I thought there was, but it doesn't seem to be here."

"Oh, phooey," Mam said from Cissy's bedroom. "This thing has frozen up again." She met us in the hall by the door. "Sorry, Pen. Take it with you. It may be just society minutes or something like that, though. Lindsey, did you find the other one? Where are your keys? Maybe it fell out of the box yesterday."

Pen put the disk in her gray leather purse and followed Mam out the door. I dug in the black canvas book bag I was using as a purse to come up with my *Buffy the Vampire Slayer* key ring.

Pen and Mam were standing in the driveway.

"So glad you stopped by," Mam said. "You be sure and let us know when you get down this way again to see Kit. Here, Lindsey, you look in the front while I check the back."

Two empty Coke cans, several crumpled gas receipts, a Springsteen CD. I almost impaled myself on Miss Augusta's conch shell sliding back out of the car.

"No disk," I told Pen.

"Nothing back here either." Mam said. "I'll send it to Dr. Colleton if we find it. You do know the way to the main road from here?"

Pen reassured her she knew where she was going. "Bye," she said. "I'll be in touch, or Kit will."

I knew Mam would be thrilled about that.

She said as much once we were inside. "Don't think I'll hold my breath waiting to hear from Kit Caldwell. But Pen is so nice. I guess that's why she can put up with Kit, although they didn't seem that buddy-buddy New Year's Eve."

"Pen can't afford to tell Kit to get lost if she wants to sell her those antiques for Hillcrest," I pointed out. "She probably has to suck up to people she doesn't like all the time."

"I suppose so," Mam said. "Don't you like Pen as a nickname? More sophisticated than Penny."

"When I was little, before I ever heard anybody pronounce Penelope, I read it in a book. I thought it was pronounced Pen-e-lope, like antelope."

"Or cantaloupe."

"Why is it that every conversation we have ends up being about food?"

"Because we were raised that way. Our mamas always talk about the next meal while we're eating the current one. They're going to be in hog heaven on this cruise. You can eat all day and night. If you don't get enough at the midnight buffet, there's pizza at two in the morning. And speaking of food"—she had the good grace to grin—"Bonnie's going to pick us up something for dinner on the way back from Charleston. She said she'd call before she headed back. Too bad she missed Pen. Don't you think Pen looks a lot younger than Kit?"

"Hard to say. Kit's not that much older than us, I don't think. Mid-forties, maybe."

"Uh-uh." Mam shook her head authoritatively. "She's older than that. She's been Botoxed. I heard her telling Sally Simmons about it, suggesting Sally come with her to a Botox party sometime. Can you imagine letting someone inject poison in your forehead?"

"Cheaper than a facelift, I hear."

"I'm not doing that either. If you're finished with the silver, you can help me with the Dickens." Mam headed back toward the dining room.

"In a sec," I said.

I checked my cell to see if there was anything on my voice mail. Nope. I dialed Mama's code. Nada.

"Why don't you call Will and see what new clues he has?" Mam said.

Not for the first time, I wondered if she had eyes in the back of her head.

"Call him yourself," I said. "Like he's going to tell either of us a darn thing. Give me one of those Dickens whatchamecallums."

She handed me Victoria Station and what appeared to be a fishmonger's shop. Excuse me, *shoppe*. Mam must have spent a fortune on this stuff over the years.

"Did you know," I asked, "that the guy who built Bleak Hall over on Edisto named it after Dickens's *Bleak House*?"

"Didn't it burn down?" Mam asked, turning on her Dustbuster to get up the remains of the fake snow on the hutch. "It's just ruins now, like Hillcrest."

"That was the second house," I said, raising my voice over

the noise. "Some yahoo pulled it down, and also Sea Cloud, which was supposed to be one of the most beautiful plantation houses in the Low Country."

Mam shut off the Dustbuster. "Uh-huh. I remember reading that somewhere, and also that Sea Cloud was named after the last two names of the couple who owned it, Seabrook and McLeod. I wonder if they were any kin to Will."

It seemed that there was just no getting away from that man.

Mam was now looking through a stack of books. "Here," she said, handing me what looked like a self-published paperback. "Bailey Pope finally finished that memoir he's been working on. I haven't read it yet, but I got stuck with it at our Sunday-school Christmas party. You know, where you play that game where you get a present and someone can take it from you? Bailey's niece had it all wrapped up in this fancy paper, and I thought it was going to be a box of candy. But there are some good pictures in there of Edisto and Indigo. There could be something in there about the McLeods."

I thumbed through the book, figuring it was better than cracking pecans and trying to separate nuts and shells while watching Cissy on tape.

Mam got to the phone before I did.

"Oh, hey, we were just talking about you."

Will?

"Are you calling for our food order?"

Bonnie.

"No! You're kidding! Are you all right? You sure? What about the car? Why didn't you call us before?"

I was standing by Mam, who interrupted Bonnie.

"Hold on. Let me tell Lindsey. Somebody tried to run Bonnie's car off the road this morning, right before the bridge. A gray truck. She thinks it was Eddie Smoak!"

chapter twelve

Floundering Around

"I could just shoot that Eddie Smoak!" Mam was still vehement four hours later. "Trying to kill my baby sister!"

"I don't think he was trying to kill me," said Bonnie, looking the picture of composure, wearing the green dress from the funeral, only with a different scarf. "I think he was just trying to scare me. He took advantage of the opportunity when he came to a spot where he could pass me and no one else was on the road. But if I'd gone off into the marsh and drowned, he probably wouldn't have cared." She hunched her shoulders, then straightened. "Really, I'm fine, Mam. Stop fussing. Here, take this." She handed over a white paper sack. "I know you said not to worry about getting something for dinner, but I couldn't resist going by Taste of the South and picking up some of their pimento cheese biscuits."

"Oh, I love these." Mam was distracted from thoughts of Bonnie's brush with death by the smell wafting from the sack.

Bonnie kicked off her heels before padding back to the kitchen in her nylons. "We sure don't need to build a fire tonight," she said. "I want to get out of these clothes, and then I want a glass of wine and some dinner." She opened the refrigerator door. "On second thought, I'll have that wine first."

"We're still figuring out dinner," Mam said as I reached into the cabinet and found three wine glasses. "It's just us three. J. T. went flounder-gigging 'cause it's so warm, and Cissy's over at Ashley's studying. Oh, good, you got a dozen. I can practically make a meal off these."

"Me, too," I said. "Just need some chocolate."

"And more wine," added Bonnie, who claims that a good Chardonnay is the only cure for PMS. Of course, grocery-store zinfandel will do in a pinch, as long as it doesn't have a screw top.

"Well, that sounds like we've got dinner covered," Mam said. "Bonnie, go change your clothes while I warm up the biscuits. There's some ham we can have. And while we're eating, we can watch Cissy's cheerleading tape from last season. Lindsey didn't get to watch it today, 'cause Pen came over. She's gone back to Philadelphia early."

As usual, Mam had her head in the fridge, presenting us with a view of her blue-jeaned rear. Admittedly trim, but still a butt. She kept right on talking while she looked for the ham. "Wait till you see how much Cissy has improved. The same can't be said for that Gates girl. She's the reason Cissy fell off the pyramid. If you put the tape on pause, you can see right where Heather starts to wobble."

Bonnie and I exchanged gagging motions.

"I want Bonnie to see the stuff we found in Bailey Pope's book," I interjected. "He can't write worth a hoot, but there are some pictures of Pinckney and some of the old ferry landing at White's Point. Go change."

"Be right back," Bonnie said.

"Lindsey, you can cue up the tape," Mam said.

Lord, she wasn't going to rest until we watched Cissy's acrobatic feats and poor Heather's literal downfall. I poured myself some more wine and looked to replenish Bonnie's, but she had taken her glass.

"Here," she said when she reappeared, proffering her glass. I filled it to the brim. "I like that T-shirt," she said. "Where did you get it?"

"Jack sent it to me for Christmas," I said. "It's this band he knows in Orlando. One guy's a lawyer, one's a professor, another's a dentist, I think. I love the name: Men with Mortgages. They trademarked it."

"You bet they did, if one of them's a lawyer." Bonnie nodded approvingly. "Here, show me those pictures," she said, taking a gulp so it wouldn't spill as she plopped onto the overstuffed sofa. "We can watch that video later, maybe when Cissy's with us."

"And we've had more wine," I said so only she could hear.

"What are you two giggling about in there?" Mam called.

"Oh, just this picture of these old-timey clothes," I said. "Cissy better hope Miss Augusta doesn't see this, or she'll have to get a new costume that looks more authentic. Or at least not so purple."

"Isn't this the front of Pinckney?" Bonnie asked. "Gosh, the trees were so small then. I wonder when it was taken."

"It doesn't say," I said. "Bailey's captions leave a lot to be desired. But look at that black man's beat-up Rebel coat. So the time frame had to be after the war. That live oak is no longer there, so maybe it was before the 1893 hurricane. There were a couple of other big storms, though, and an earthquake, too. So it's hard to tell."

"I wonder what he's signing?" That was the lawyer in Bonnie asking.

"Most freedmen couldn't write."

Bonnie peered at the picture. "He could sign his name, probably. I suppose the plantation owner could have been paying him some wages. I'd date it in the late 1800s. Who was the owner of Pinckney during that time?"

"Oh, that would have been Theophilus Pinckney. He married a Bailey from Oak Hall," Margaret Ann said from the kitchen. She sure didn't need a hearing aid. "A lot of Manigaults worked for him after the war. So that man could be a Manigault, or he could have come from Oak Hall or one of the smaller plantations. Bradford gave a presentation at the historical-society meeting last fall about former slaves on Indigo who became tenant farmers."

"Is that where Freedmen's Village came from?" Bonnie asked.

"Could be," I said. "Or it might have started during the war, when Sherman sent all those former slaves here and to Edisto for the Union army to take care of."

"Well, let me take this book with me when I go back to Charleston tomorrow." She saw my look of surprise. "Mam didn't tell you I had to change my flight to Friday?"

"No, it was all about Eddie trying to kill you. Y'all didn't finish?"

"One more meeting." She sounded exasperated. "Oh, it's okay.

I'm ready to go home and see Tom and the boys, but after my run-in with Eddie"—she grimaced—"I didn't have time to check those permits. I'll go tomorrow, and then I thought I'd run by and see Marietta. Maybe she can tell us more about this picture. I might go by Talbots, too. I'm getting tired of these clothes."

"Oh, and here are some more pictures," I said, fetching the box we'd retrieved from Pinckney. "The historical society's been collecting them from families on the island. They're going to do one of those books, Mam told me."

"*Images of America*," Mam announced, joining us on the sofa. Suddenly, her back end didn't seem so small. Bonnie and I had to shift to give her room. "That's the name of the series. They all have the same format, paperback with lots of photos of towns and communities, showing the history. There's one for Edisto, I know, and one for Walterboro. Anyway, Bradford was so busy with his book that Beth has been doing most of the work, trying to identify the people in the pictures and date them."

"You mean like this one?" I held up a little black-and-white snapshot of a crew-cut, gap-toothed kid proudly holding up a string of fish on a backyard dock. It could have been the subject of a Norman Rockwell painting. "This just says 'Catch of the Day' on the back."

"That's the problem," Mam said. "Some people turned in old pictures with no names or just first names. This looks like it was taken in the fifties, but who's the little boy? And where and when was it taken?"

"Let me see," said Bonnie. "It's so faded it's hard to pick out details."

"You can see more in this one, even though it's older," I said, looking at a sepia picture of a girl of about twelve or thirteen holding a baby. A curly-headed moppet with a serious expression stood next to her. Even though the whole picture was the color of iced tea, I could see the lace-trimmed dresses were white. I turned it over. The year *1919* was written in faded brown ink on the back. "You could call this 'An Old-Fashioned Girl.' Or girls. I think this toddler is a girl, but sometimes they put little boys in dresses, and didn't cut their hair short until they were older. Aunt Cora has that picture of Carl Ed from when he was little, and he looks just like a girl."

"I think it's a girl, too," Bonnie said, leaning in for a closer look. "But that baby could be a boy or a girl. Aren't those steps in the background at Pinckney?"

"Looks like it," Mam said. "That older girl looks sort of familiar. But after you look at a lot of these period pictures, they all start looking familiar. But if it is Pinckney, I'm surprised Beth didn't pick up on it, and especially Bradford. I wonder if Miss Augusta's even seen it. Put it back in that envelope, and we'll carry it back to Pinckney tomorrow. It's tape time."

"How 'bout dinnertime?" I said quickly. "We can take paper plates out on the dock and see the moon. Come on. It's such a pretty night."

And it was. Our sneakers echoed softly on the weathered planking of the long, straight dock. The tide was low, so there wasn't even a breeze. It was almost like spring, except there were no bugs, thank goodness. Still, you could smell a faint odor of pluff mud, sort of like a school locker room. Or that was what outsiders said, wrinkling up their noses. It was such a part of Indigo and home that we hardly noticed, and we certainly didn't let it ruin our appetites.

We ate in rare silence, content for the moment with our food and the calm. Bonnie's wine glass plinked as she set it down on the dock. I leaned back against one piling while Mam swung her feet over the end of the dock, staring down at the water with its black and silver shadows. A whippoorwill called out once, then again, this time farther off.

A loud crack broke the silence.

"Your dock is falling apart," I said, lazily brushing biscuit crumbs into the dark water.

There was another crack. This time, I felt wood splinter close to my hand.

"Gun!" Bonnie shouted.

"Get down!" I said, yanking at Mam, who, like an idiot, was starting to stand up.

Another crack.

"In the creek!" I yelled, grabbing Mam's waist and shoving her off the dock.

I rolled after her and gasped as I hit the cold water. Bonnie splashed in next to us. I pulled a sputtering Mam by one arm and reached for a shell-encrusted piling with the other.

"Here," I said, pulling her underneath the dock. I winced as I felt barnacles below the water line scraping my leg. "Hang on to the piling. Bonnie, are you okay?"

"Don't sharks feed at night?" Bonnie asked, a catch in her throat.

"Not in the creek," Mam said. "I'm more worried about the sharks on land. The ones with guns."

We tensed, waiting for another shot to come out of the darkness. The moon had vanished behind a cloud, and the night was full of unknown shadows.

"I can't believe it," Mam said. She lowered her voice to a loud whisper. "You suppose it's Eddie come to finish us off? 'Course, how would he even know we were out here? How would anyone know?"

"Well, whoever it is knows now," Bonnie said. "We've made enough noise. Mam, I think I've lost one of your moccasins."

"Which moccasins? I hope you weren't wearing those new ones Mama got me for Christmas. She gave you some, too. Why aren't you wearing yours?"

"Because I didn't bring them. If I can't get this one back, I'll mail you mine. But the water's pretty shallow, so I can probably find it."

I felt the water moving as she made a sweeping motion with one leg.

"Be careful you don't lose the other one," Mam said. "I don't see why you had to put on my new moccasins when—"

"Shush," I said. "I think I hear a boat motor."

"Maybe it's J. T.," said Bonnie.

"Lord, yes, I'd know that loud sputtering anywhere," said Mam, letting out a sigh of relief.

A light appeared just around the creek bend as the sound of the motor grew even louder, drowning out whatever it was Mam was saying to Bonnie. More about her moccasin, I bet. There were two figures in the boat. As the heavy beam of a flashlight scanned the marsh, I could see J. T. in the stern and Will wielding the light.

J. T. slowed the boat almost to a standstill upon spotting us, quieting the engine. I couldn't see the expression on Will's face because he was behind the light, but J. T. was his usual unperturbed self as he looked at us hanging onto the underside of the dock.

"Margaret Ann, you usually save moonlight swims for me," he drawled. " 'Course, you're not usually wearing any clothes."

Bonnie and I squeezed hands underwater, trying not to snicker.

"Well, it *is* January, J. T.," Mam said.

"Ouch!" I said as Mam applied hydrogen peroxide to my knee, where a particularly vicious barnacle had sliced through a worn place on my jeans. They were now in the washer, along with the rest of our sodden clothes. We'd all taken quick showers, and I had borrowed sweatpants and a Citadel T-shirt from Mam. She and Bonnie had put on their nightgowns and robes.

"Stop being such a baby," Mam said. "Oyster shells and barnacles can infect your skin. You don't want a scar, do you? You know, you can't stitch an oyster cut, and a barnacle's just as bad."

"But not as bad as a bullet," Will said. He dropped two bullets and a waterlogged moccasin on the kitchen table next to Mam's first-aid supplies. "J. T. and I dug these bullets out of the dock. So maybe you girls weren't imagining things."

I started to say something, but Bonnie was there first.

"How dare you think we made up something as serious as this?" She fixed Will with a look that could have frozen the flounder he'd just gigged. "As if we don't know the sound of a gunshot when we hear one. For heaven's sake, I live in D.C. A major crime capital!"

"What I want to know," said J. T., "is who was shooting a gun on the creek."

"And why," Will said. "Did you ever stop to think that maybe, just maybe, it wasn't some teen showing off the new rifle he got for Christmas? That all those questions you've been asking about

Bradford Bentley—don't interrupt me—might have pissed somebody off? This isn't a game, or some TV show. I told you to stay out of it, and I mean it."

He picked up the bullets and walked out, letting the screen door slam behind him.

"J. T.," Mam began.

"Don't start with me, Margaret Ann," J. T. said.

He followed Will outside, leaving the three of us in the kitchen. Chloe, no doubt feeling the tension in the air, whined uncertainly, looking at us for reassurance.

Mam patted the dog's head absently. "I was just going to ask him if he wanted a pimento cheese biscuit."

"Uh, Will?" He was heading toward his truck, but I caught up with him. "I need to tell you something."

After a quick consultation, Mam, Bonnie, and I had decided we best let Will know about Eddie. Actually, they'd decided that I should tell him.

"What is it?" He stopped and leaned against the CR-V.

"It's about Eddie Smoak."

I had his attention now. I gave him a quick recap of our visit to Hillcrest and then quickly told him about Bonnie nearly being run off the road.

"She's sure it was Eddie?"

"Pretty sure. He has all those bumper stickers on the back of his truck. Will, what's going on out at Hillcrest? Does he really work for Miller?"

"Yes, he's some sort of guard, although I don't know why Miller and Luis"—he looked at me pointedly—"had to hire a redneck thug like Eddie to watch over some weeds and collards.

Did you see anything odd when you were out there?"

"Just Eddie."

Will sighed. "Is there anything else you and your cousins haven't told me?"

I didn't think Aunt Cora and the candlestick counted, so I shook my head.

"Okay. I'm going to go check and see if I can find out Mr. Eddie Smoak's whereabouts. I think it might be a good idea if you stay here tonight, until we get this straightened out."

"Mam's already making up the couch. I've got some more Coke in the car I want to get out. I've drunk all hers, and I'll need it in the morning."

"You and your Coke." His voice softened. "Oh, Lindsey, what am I going to do with you?"

"I don't know that I've asked you to do anything with me."

The light in the CR-V came on. I wondered if Will was going to kiss me. I wondered if Mam and Bonnie could see us through the window.

"What's this?"

"A conch shell. We picked it up out at Pinckney yesterday. Cissy says it's usually in the attic, but she found it by the back steps. . . ."

From Will's expression, it looked as if Bradford Bentley had been conked on the head—literally.

chapter thirteen

Three for Tea

I woke up with a headache. Too much wine, too little sleep, too many odd dreams, and now too much noise coming from the kitchen.

"Mam, what in the heck are you doing?" Bonnie's voice was sleepy. "And how can you see to make a grocery list with just that light from the stove?"

"Shh." One of Mam's loud whispers. "You'll wake up Lindsey. And I'm not making a grocery list, but I need to do that, too. There's enough milk for cereal this morning, but we're low on orange juice, and Lindsey drank all the Coke except for those cans she brought in last night. No, I'm compiling a list of suspects. This side is for those with opportunity, and this side is for those with motive. I might have to continue that list on the back, 'cause it's lots longer. Although just not liking someone really isn't a good motive for murder. Not like love or money or revenge."

"Or being crazy, which is what you are," Bonnie mumbled. "It's still dark outside. In fact, it's practically the middle of the night."

"Well, I had to pee, and once I wake up, I'm up," Mam said. "I don't need any caffeine to jump-start my day, but by all means help yourself. I turned on the coffee maker for J. T. when I came down awhile ago. And you didn't have to get up so early."

"I heard some gosh-awful racket from outside. Sounded like metal being thrown in the street."

I had heard it, too, but when Chloe didn't bark, I'd rolled over and dozed back off.

"Raccoons," Mam said now. "J. T. bought a coon-proof trash can, and they get so frustrated they can't get the top off, they turn the can over. I found it halfway in the road one morning last week, but the lid was still on it."

"Mm." Bonnie must be preoccupied with her coffee.

I thought about getting up, but it seemed like too much effort. Maybe if I put one of the sofa pillows over my head, I could go back to sleep. But now that Mam had a sounding board, she was off and running.

"I could put the tourists and all the history people from out of town on the list, but they didn't have any personal connection to Bradford."

"How do you know?" Bonnie asked.

"Well, it stands to reason we'd have heard about it by now—or Lindsey would have."

Why me?

Bonnie echoed my thoughts: "Why would Lindsey know?"

"Because Will would have told her, or she'd have wormed it out of him," Mam said. "In case you haven't noticed, dear sister, there's something going on between those two. I think our cousin is falling for the lawman, and from the way he looks at her when she's not looking at him, he's falling right back."

Uh-oh. This is what I got for pretending to be asleep. But I was wide awake now.

"You really think so?" Bonnie sounded bemused. "Now that you mention it, she was awful quick to go out there last night and tell him about Eddie. And I was the one that was almost road kill."

Wait a minute. That was hardly fair. Mam had volunteered me because I was the only one who had on shoes—an old pair of Cissy's Nikes while mine were drying out.

"See?" Mam was triumphant. "I bet my bottom dollar something's going on there, or soon will be. But I'm not sure it's a good idea, him being on the rebound. No, wait, Chloe, don't go in there. You'll wake up . . ."

She was too late. Chloe had discovered me on the couch and was showing her delight with pants of morning dog breath. Ugh.

"Chloe, get down." Margaret Ann was standing over me. "Sorry she woke you up. But now that you're awake, you can help us work on our list."

"What list?" Like I didn't know. I listened to Mam's explanation with suitable grogginess. "All right, all right." I yawned for real. "Let me get up and get some Coke, and I'll look at that list of yours."

"I don't see how you can drink Coca-Cola this early in the morning," Mam said.

"It's because it's this early in the morning," I said, putting ice in a glass. "You know I don't drink coffee. A girl's got to wake up somehow. And why are we up so early anyway? It's still dark outside."

"It'll be light soon," Bonnie said, pouring another cup of coffee. "J. T. and Cissy will be down in a minute. I heard the shower running."

"First bell at the high school's at eight," Mam said. She put boxes of Cheerios and Raisin Bran on the table. "And J. T. always allows at least forty-five minutes, in case the drawbridge is up."

She handed me a piece of paper torn from a notepad I'd put in her Christmas stocking. It featured a sassy cat at the top and the caption, "I don't do Mousework."

This must be the famous list. Beth Chesnut. Henry Colleton. Pen Upchurch. Kit Caldwell. Miller Caldwell. Sally Simmons. Ray Simmons. Pinck Townsend. Jamie Townsend. Eddie Smoak . . .

"Miss Augusta, Marietta, Aunt Cora, Cissy, Jimmy," I read aloud. "Mam, you have lost your marbles. Why don't you put our names down there, too?"

"I was just trying to be objective," Mam said defensively. "We weren't there, but all these people were, or at least I think they could have been. Of course, I'm going to cross off most of them. They had opportunity but not motive. Like Cissy."

"What about me?" asked Cissy, breezing into the kitchen.

"Your mother is considering you for a starring role in 'Murder at Pinckney Plantation,' " I said darkly.

"Cool," said Cissy. "Can Jimmy be in it, too? Hey, we need some more orange juice."

"Tell your mother to put it on the list," Bonnie said. "The grocery list."

"Oh, I don't know," I interjected. "Mam might want to put

O.J. on both lists."

The potholder she threw at me knocked over a cereal box, spilling Cheerios to the floor. Chloe was thrilled.

"I still don't see why Will thinks someone was shooting at us," Mam said. While Bonnie and I had slowly woken to the day, she had unloaded the dishwasher, gotten Cissy and J. T. fed and on the road, cleared the table, swept up the Cheerios Chloe somehow missed, reloaded the dishwasher, watered the poinsettias, and made out her grocery list. Now, she was going over her list of suspects again. "I don't see any of these people shooting at us, except for Eddie. Probably some teenager got a new rifle for Christmas and was just showing off for his friends. I told Will that last night. And I'm pretty sure that's what J. T. thinks."

"But there's a good many people out here on the creek," Bonnie said. "Whoever it was could have hit somebody."

"Like us," I said.

We had considered these same questions the night before, but by daylight—well, almost daylight—it seemed even more ridiculous to think someone had been aiming at the three of us.

"Maybe Will's right that someone wanted to scare us," Bonnie said. The lawyer in her always wants to play devil's advocate. "Maybe all our questions have struck a nerve."

"With who?" Mam snorted. "All we've done is talk to some old ladies. I don't see Miss Maudie toting a shotgun, or Miss Augusta, who, by the way, is expecting you and me, Lindsey, to help her take down her Christmas decorations today. The painters are supposed to start at Pinckney tomorrow, or maybe it's the carpenters redoing some of the front porch. I can't remember."

"If it's carpenters, they need to work on the attic stairs," I said. "But you can bet they'll show up on their schedule, not Miss Augusta's."

"No, they like working at Pinckney, 'cause she pays them extra," Mam said. "She wants to have the place all pretty and ready to reopen February 1st, just like the Charleston plantations. If we don't get a hard freeze, there may even be some camellias left."

"Don't hold your breath," Bonnie said. "I had the radio on when I woke up, and there's already a cold front on the way. The temperature's supposed to plummet starting about the middle of the day."

"I hope Cissy took her coat," Mam said. "Lindsey, you need to go home and feed Peaches so we can get going. Wear something old and warm, because you know she's going to have us putting stuff underneath the house and in the attic, and it's already like an icebox out there. Finish your Coke and get a move on. You, too, Bonnie, if you're going to the courthouse. We got places to go and people to see."

"Yes, ma'am, Mam!" Bonnie and I chorused.

Mam definitely didn't need caffeine. On the other hand, if someone gave her a Mountain Dew, we might have world peace by midday.

"Put those ornaments over here, Lindsey," Mam directed. "They need to be wrapped in tissue paper before they go in the boxes."

"Where are the boxes?" I asked. "No, don't tell me. They're downstairs." I groaned. It would be about my fifth trip down the narrow wooden stairs to the cold basement. At least it was only one flight. Although the Christmas decorations were stored in the attic, someone had shown the good sense to temporarily set the empty boxes closer by.

Mam's dictatorial manner had continued at Pinckney, especially after she got a look at Miss Augusta, who was frailer than ever and kept twisting her hands.

"I am so glad you girls are here," she'd said. "Every time I start to do something, I can't seem to get finished. I am so, so"—she searched for the word—"rattled or distracted, that's it. And I don't know how we're going to get all this done without Marietta. Did I tell you the doctors think she's some better today? Her vitamins are good. I mean, her vitals."

Margaret Ann and I had exchanged glances. This wasn't the Miss Augusta we knew. Her hair needed combing, and she'd missed a buttonhole on her navy-blue cardigan, so the sweater hung crooked. She seemed relieved when Mam took over, settling her in a chair at the dining-room table so she could dismantle the centerpiece, separating the fruit from the candles. We'd started in on the garlands in the front hall, pitching the browning boughs into trash bags.

Now, three hours later, pine needles littered the wood floors and heirloom rugs, but we were almost finished. The two Christmas trees—a Douglas fir in the front hall and a spruce pine in the parlor—looked sad with just tinsel strands hanging from their denuded branches. I made the mistake of saying so.

"Do, Lindsey," Mam said, standing on a stepstool and unhooking an overlooked star. "They're just Christmas trees that have been oohed and aahed over for more than a month by all the visitors. You act like they have feelings or something. You get this way every year after the holidays. At least you've got something to look forward to this year."

"What do you mean?"

"I mean I saw the way Will was looking at you last night. And don't tell me I'm imagining things. Bonnie saw it, too. What I want to know is how long it's been going on."

Forever, I thought. I wanted to tell her everything, all the feelings I'd kept dammed up over the years. Will. Darlene. Dennis. Will. But I wasn't ready to say anything yet to anybody, even to Mam or Bonnie. Whatever was going on between Will and me was still too tenuous to stand up to scrutiny. And it was complicated, as much by the present as the past. There were other people to consider, like Jimmy, and the logistics of a long-distance relationship. Things Will and I hadn't even talked about.

"There's nothing going on," I said stiffly. "Will and I are just friends."

"If you say so, but he looks like a man with more than friendship on his mind."

"How about murder?" I said, wrapping the crystal star in tissue paper.

"Murder?" said Miss Augusta from the doorway. "What on earth are you girls talking about?"

"Oh, just an old movie that was on TV the other night," Mam said quickly. "That one where two strangers are on a train. What's it called, Lindsey?"

"*Strangers on a Train.*"

"Hitchcock," Miss Augusta said. "He directed the movie. Patricia Highsmith wrote the book. You two girls want some tea?"

Miss Augusta was Miss Augusta again.

"That sounds good," Mam said. "I'll fix it."

"No, I'll do it while you finish up in here." Miss Augusta headed briskly for the kitchen.

"She's better," I said. "Maybe we can ask her about those pictures."

Mam's cell phone sounded from her purse on the table.

"You get it, Lindsey. I see another ornament back here."

It was Bonnie. "Oh, good, I'm glad I got you," she said. "Are y'all still at Pinckney?"

"Yep, it's going pretty well. Where are you?" I mouthed "Bonnie" at Mam.

"I'm on Bee's Ferry Road, heading toward 17. Listen, I just wanted to make sure you were going to be there awhile yet, and I'll stop by. I found some stuff at the courthouse, but then I really got the goods from Marietta."

"Marietta?"

"Yep," Bonnie said. "She's doing lots better. I stopped by, and she'd been moved to a regular room. She was sitting up in bed complaining about the food, said she didn't want any more red Jell-O and cold scrambled eggs. She said, 'I don't think a real chicken laid those eggs.' Sounded just like herself, even if she doesn't remember what happened."

"Hold on," I said. Mam was trying to wrest the phone from me. I held it up in the air and started climbing the stairs. "Marietta's better, and Bonnie's on her way here," I told her. "I'll be off the phone in just a sec, but you best go see that Miss Augusta's not burning down the house meanwhile." Mam made a face but surprisingly didn't argue with me. "Okay, Bonnie. I'm back. Mam and Miss Augusta are making tea."

"Well, we may all need something stronger than tea before this day is over. There was also a slave cemetery on Pinckney. Marietta remembers her granny taking her there when she was a little girl. Said she'd forgotten all about it and didn't reckon she could find it now, 'cause it was all overgrown even back then, but that there were some wooden crosses and shells on the graves. She remembers because she picked one up because it was pretty, and her granny made her put it back. Said it belonged to her grandmama, and how they buried her at night. There wasn't any other time, because they were working from dawn to dusk. 'Wasn't any free time, 'cause folks then weren't free.' Marietta said those were her granny's exact words."

"Goodness," I said. "We'll have to call the South Carolina archives-and-history people and see what we need to do next. I know there are all sorts of regulations about preserving old graveyards, even those that weren't slave cemeteries. Remember all that fuss at the College of Charleston when they found there was a graveyard near where they were going to put the new library?"

"Yes, and there's a little family cemetery near that mall over in Summerville. The family wouldn't let them move it, and the builders or the DOT had to redo the entrance to Wal-Mart. I'll tell you more when I see y'all, but no wonder Ray and Pinck are worried. They might have their permits from dee-heck for water easement, but trying to develop a gated community on a slave cemetery is something else altogether."

DOT. That would be the Department of Transportation. Dee-heck was DHEC. I couldn't remember what the letters stood for, but it was the agency in charge of permits for docks and so forth. Every time homeowners said to heck with DHEC and started putting up docks on their own, DHEC somehow heard about it. Developers wondered if they employed psychics. Nosy neighbors was more like it.

"So much for Magnolia Cay," Bonnie said. "I'm hanging up, 'cause I'm coming up on that spot where you're not going to be able to hear me." Already, there was static.

"Okay. You done good. A real slave cemetery. Imagine that. We'll have to take Marietta some barbecue. Bye."

"What's this about taking Marietta barbecue?" Miss Augusta said. "When I talked to those doctors this A.M., they said she'd probably have to be in the hospital at least another week, and then the rehab center for her hip. Now, I admit she looks pretty good for someone who looks terrible, but barbecue! She might just as well ask for a heart attack."

Mam passed me a cup of tea Miss Augusta had poured.

"Miss Augusta, was there ever a slave cemetery on Pinckney? Graves separate from those up near your family?"

"There might have been, I suppose," she said. "You know, Pinck asked me that same thing back this fall, and I told him to ask Bradford." She stopped and shook her head. "I still can't believe Bradford's gone. He was such a nice man, and smart. What he knew about Low Country history! Lindsey, dear, you would have liked him so much. Everybody did. It's just such a pity."

"Yes'm," I said. "He sounded like quite a historian." I wasn't enough of a hypocrite to continue the praise. Obviously, Miss Augusta didn't see or chose to ignore how Bradford Bentley had rubbed most people the wrong way. "Did he ever get back to you on the slave cemetery?"

"No, I forgot all about it, what with the holidays coming and so much to do out here." She took a sip of tea. "If there was one, though, it could be quite a tourist draw. It's not every plantation that can advertise a slave cemetery. I'll have to ask Pinck if Bradford ever told him anything."

I cut my eyes at Mam, who nodded. It was typical of Miss Augusta to be totally focused on tourists and not even wonder why her nephew, famously disinterested in history or anything that didn't concern his bank account or golf game, wanted to know about a slave cemetery. It was even more typical for her not to see that the descendants of the Pinckney slaves might want to know where their family members were buried. And heaven forbid that Marietta might actually know more than her pet historian.

But we'd wait for Bonnie to fill us in before we went any farther in that direction.

"What kind of tea is this?" It tasted like wet weeds with a little cinnamon thrown in. I put my cup down.

"It's some kind of spiced tea that Beth gave me for Christmas," Miss Augusta said. "Supposed to be soothing. Personally, I prefer Earl Grey—Twinings, if I run out of Fortnum & Mason. Belinda brings it to me from London. But I couldn't seem to find any today. I hope this is all right with you girls."

"It's fine," Mam said, downing hers quickly, like it was medicine. "Very fortifying. Before we get started again, we found some pictures in the office the other day. Didn't know if you'd seen them. I think they're for that book Aunt Cora and Beth have been working on."

"I really haven't paid much mind to that little project," Miss Augusta said dismissively. "I was helping Bradford with the Pinckney book. It was going to be quite an important work. Scholarly, of course, but with popular appeal as well."

"I heard Henry Colleton was going to finish it," Mam said.

"Yes," Miss Augusta said. "That's the plan now." She didn't sound too confident.

"Don't you think he can do it?" I asked.

"Hmm?" Miss Augusta had a faraway look in her eyes. Maybe she was imagining the Pinckney name on the *New York Times* bestseller list. And maybe a movie deal after that. Or "Pinckney: The Musical!"

The vision of hoop-skirted dancers twirling Pinckney purple parasols made my stomach churn. Or maybe it was the tea. Beth's idea of spiced tea was not my, well, cup of tea.

"You said something about some pictures?" Miss Augusta asked. "Unless they had to do with Pinckney, I was letting Beth deal with them."

"There's one that I think was taken here. It's dated 1919, but there's no names on it." I fished the sepia print out of the envelope I'd put in my combination book bag and purse.

Miss Augusta looked surprised at the picture. "You say this was in the office box?"

I nodded. "Yes, it was with a few others, but they were all more recent. It was taken here, wasn't it? Do you recognize it?"

Miss Augusta considered the photograph, holding it first at arm's length, then up close. "Yes, it is Pinckney. It must have just been turned in. Otherwise, I'm sure Bradford or Beth would have brought it to my attention." She looked put out. "But I can't say that I recognize these children. Maybe some visitors? You know, I didn't come to live here until after my poor mother passed away when I was a little girl. Papa wanted to keep me with him, but what with his military career to consider, it was just impossible. I lived with my mother's cousin Elizabeth in Richmond for a while, but she had quite a large family of her own. So Papa arranged for me to live here at Pinckney with his older sister. Aunt Letitia was a widow, lost her husband and her only son in the Spanish flu epidemic. I came to her when I was five." She put the photo on the table. "I'll add this to the Pinckney collection I have upstairs."

"Maybe Aunt Cora will know who the little girls are. Or Miss Maudie," Mam said. "We're supposed to see Aunt Cora tonight. Stick it back in the envelope, Lindsey." She turned to Miss Augusta. "What else do you need us to do before Bonnie gets here?"

"Oh, let's see." Miss Augusta was beginning to look frazzled again. "Why don't we just take these boxes of garland up to the attic and call it a day?"

We? She meant Margaret Ann and me.

I balanced two boxes on my knee, and Mam added a third to the stack. They weren't heavy, but their size made the load awkward.

"You'll have to lead the way, 'cause I can't see," I said. "You've just got those two."

We marched single file up the front stairs to the second floor, then turned down the hall. Miss Augusta followed with the red sateen bow from the parlor wreath. I tried not to think of the last time we'd been up here, and how we were now walking the very floor where Bradford had died. My stomach lurched. Although I was sure the blood was long gone, I was just as glad the boxes hid my view.

Apparently, the door to the attic stairs was already open, because Mam didn't have to stop. The stairs seemed sturdy enough as I followed her up. I hoped the crunch I heard under my foot was stray Christmas garland and not a palmetto bug.

As Mam reached the top, I turned my head and called over my shoulder, "Miss Augusta, is there anywhere special we need to stack these boxes?"

But she had vanished behind the closing door. It thudded shut, and there was a loud click.

chapter fourteen

At a Loss for Words

"Miss Augusta?" I called, setting down the boxes. I went back down the attic stairs and turned the knob. The door was definitely locked.

"Miss Augusta!" Louder this time. "Margaret Ann and I are still in the attic. We need you to let us out. Miss Augusta?"

No answer. I beat my fist on the heavy door. What in the world was going on with her? I'd thought she was back to being herself, but now she apparently had reverted to the day's earlier state of confusion.

"Mam," I called up the stairs. "You're not going to believe this. Miss Augusta's locked us in."

"No way," Mam said. She looked down at me. "Try the knob again."

It wouldn't budge.

"Here, let me." Mam descended the stairs and twisted the knob, then shouted through the door: "*Miss Augusta! Let us out!*"

"Geez, Mam," I said, "I think you've deafened me." I shook my head to stop the ringing and backed up a couple of stairs. It was a tight fit with the two of us and the banister. "Lord, the whole island ought to be running to our rescue. I can't believe she didn't hear that. What's with her?"

"I don't know. Maybe she's sick." Mam looked as perplexed as I felt. She took a deep breath. "Let's go back upstairs. I'm starting to feel claustrophobic. You know how I get."

I did. Neither of us is much on closed-in spaces, but Mam is much worse. She hates airplanes, although that's probably more a feeling of not being in control. Maybe if she could sit next to the pilot . . .

"Bonnie will be here soon," I noted. "Meantime, we can go see if there's a window we can open."

"Hardly," Mam said, surveying the possibilities from the top of the stairs. "Even if we can get to them, they're going to be the devil to open."

I looked at the high dormer windows, grime clinging to the leaded glass, corners laced with cobwebs. Mam was right. They obviously hadn't been opened in years. Oh, well . . . Bonnie would come looking for us before long, or Miss Augusta would suddenly regain her hearing.

"Lindsey?"

"Mm."

The attic, which ran the length of the house, was surprisingly empty. I had hoped for big steamer trunks with rusty locks that would nonetheless open at a touch, revealing vintage lace dresses or packets of old letters tied with faded ribbon.

"I don't feel so good." Margaret Ann was leaning against the wall next to the stairs, her face pale and beads of sweat on her forehead.

"You don't look so good," I said appraisingly. "Are you sick on your stomach? Anything hurt?"

"No," she said. "I just feel sort of lightheaded and weird. Maybe I better sit down."

She looked like she might fall down any second. I guided her to a nearby chair, only to see that someone had removed the cane seat and attached a tin bucket in its place. But Mam didn't seem to care, or even realize, that she was now sitting on some makeshift version of a Porta-Potty.

"My mouf," she said.

"What about your mouth?"

"Numb." She closed her eyes, slumping.

"Mam! Don't you go and faint on me. I'll never be able to pry your butt out of that bucket. Sit up straight." I knelt in front of her. "Mam, look at me."

She opened her eyes. "Lindsey?"

Good, she knew me. "It's going to be okay," I told her, hoping I sounded more confident than I felt. This was something other than claustrophobia. "You just sit right here and lean your head back. I'm going to see if I can get us out of here."

Back down the stairs. I really pounded on the door this time. "Miss Augusta? Miss Augusta?" I was yelling now. "Let us out! Margaret Ann's sick!"

I twisted the knob, but it didn't give a bit. Maybe if I could find a coat hanger, I could pick the lock. Except there wasn't a keyhole. Up here, Miss Augusta hadn't made any attempt at installing authentic reproductions. This was a modern deadbolt.

A Phillips-head screwdriver. Even I knew how to use one of those. Maybe I could take the whole lock off. Back up the stairs.

"How you doin', Mam?"

She looked at me glassily. She was still pale and perspiring, but her breathing was even. Her eyelids drooped. "Wanna sweep."

"No, you can't sleep. Gotta stay awake and help me. I don't suppose you have a screwdriver on you."

She made a small attempt at a smile.

There was nothing that resembled a toolbox in sight, or anything that might be used as a screwdriver or a crowbar. An old birdcage was not going to make it as a battering ram, nor was the naked dress dummy bearing silent witness in one corner. The pasteboard boxes neatly stacked by the infamous cage were equally useless. And the attic was devoid of furnishings, save for Mam's chair.

"Hang in there, kiddo."

I looked again at the windows. They probably were painted shut, but maybe if I could find a chair to stand on—preferably one with a seat—I could get a window open and crawl out on the roof. Forget my fear of heights, this was turning into a real emergency. Still, even if I did manage to get to the roof—those windows were mighty small—there wasn't anyone around to hear me call for help except Miss Augusta, who apparently had turned off her hearing aid, was sick, or was completely off her rocker.

All the phones were downstairs, including my cell. The keys to the CR-V were in my jeans pocket, but it wasn't like I could do a Harry Potter and levitate it three stories. Maybe if there was a tree . . .

I took a deep breath. "Mam, honey, I'm going to have to borrow that chair."

If I dragged it beneath a window and balanced some of those boxes on it, I might could haul myself high enough to see a convenient limb. It would be like when we were kids and played Swiss Family Robinson in Nanny's giant dogwood.

"Come on, Mam. Let's move you over here, and you can rest against the nice wall."

As I knelt, she slumped against me, her chin on my shoulder. "Aghoth," she lisped in my ear.

"What?"

"A ghoth," she said.

A ghost?

Was she starting to hallucinate? I gently leaned her back in the chair, then looked over my shoulder toward the corner of the attic, where her eyes were focused. The cage crouched in the shadows. I heard a creak, and a whisper of cold air brushed by me. A shadow shifted. I shivered involuntarily and felt the hair rise on the back of my neck. Just someone walking over my grave. The shadow moved again.

Aunt Cora!

She came to my side and bent over Margaret Ann, whose eyes had closed again.

"What has she had to eat?" she asked me.

"Nothing that I know of," I said, finally exhaling. "She drank some spiced tea awhile ago with me and Miss Augusta."

"I'm pretty sure she's having an allergic reaction of some kind." Aunt Cora looked concerned but calm. "We need to get her to a doctor right away." She put her hand on Margaret Ann's forehead. "Honey, can you hear me? You need to wake up. You're going to be just fine." Her voice was low and soothing. "Lindsey's going to help me get you out of here."

"But we're locked in," I said. "Miss Augusta might be sick, too, because she turned the key and didn't answer when I called her. I beat on the door and everything. I was going to see if I could maybe get out one of the windows."

"The cage," Aunt Cora said.

"What?"

"Here, help me get her up. There's a secret passage down to under the house. We can get outside from there."

Really, this was getting surreal, like something out of a mystery novel. Nancy Drew's hidden staircase. "Nancy Drew and the Haunted Plantation," maybe.

"Lindsey!" Aunt Cora snapped. "Take her arm. You're going to have to carry most of her weight. I've got a flashlight and will go first. It's very narrow, though, and there's one step missing down near the bottom. I hurt my shoulder when I slipped going over it last week. I'll tell you when we get to it."

Margaret Ann slumped against me again, but at least she was standing. Sort of.

"Come on, Mam," I said. "We're going for a little walk. That's right."

Slowly, we made our way across the attic. Mam was unsteady, like she'd had too much to drink. Well, this was some party, all right.

Aunt Cora shone her flashlight into the gloom, spotlighting a small opening in the wall. She shoved a large cardboard box aside and ducked into the darkness. "Be careful. It's steep."

No kidding. Aunt Cora's flashlight showed a downward flight leading to a midnight blackness. It was like going into a tomb.

Mam took one bleary look and moaned.

The last thing we needed was for her claustrophobia to really kick in. "It's okay, Mam. Just lean on me. We're going to go down these stairs now. There, that's good."

One thing about the stairs' narrowness was that Mam and I were wedged so tightly we couldn't possibly fall. We might get stuck, though. The walls were crumbling brick and mortar that snagged the shoulders of my sweatshirt. I turned my body so Mam was draped over me. I tentatively located the next step, dragging her with me. Her hair, damp with perspiration, fell across my face. It smelled of shampoo and pine. Did they still make Clairol Herbal Essence?

Aunt Cora's silhouetted head bobbed below us. At least it was cool in here, maybe even cold. Cold as a grave. Stop it, I told myself. Be brave. Think of Nancy Drew, Indiana Jones, Buffy. As we inched downward, I wondered how long the staircase had been here, and who had used it. Pinckneys hiding from marauding soldiers? Slaves being smuggled off the island and north toward freedom? A Southern belle determined to meet her Yankee lover? Well, not in a hoop skirt.

"We're coming to that step I told you about," Aunt Cora said. "You stop here and let me get across it, and then I'll shine the light so you can see. How's Margaret Ann?"

"Heavy," I said. "I think she had too many Christmas cookies. But we'll make it."

When I saw the chasm left by the missing step, I wasn't so sure. For one person, it wasn't so bad, but for two, one of whom could hardly walk, it was going to be a challenge. I could just see us falling and taking Aunt Cora with us, the three of us lying in a tangled heap in the bowels of Pinckney. Still, if our eighty-something aunt could make the hop, Mam and I could do it, too.

"Okay, Mam," I said. "Look at me. Don't look down. That's

right. Now, I want you to brace yourself against the wall, and together we're going to take one giant step forward. I'll tell you when to put your foot down. There, that's it. Lift your leg up. Good girl. Now."

I let out a breath as we crossed the space. The stair rocked when we landed on it, then steadied.

"Not too much further," Cora said. "Six, no seven steps and we're there."

It seemed an eternity before we reached the bottom. Aunt Cora shone her light on a door that opened into the back of a closet, which in turn opened into the basement underneath the stairs to the kitchen. I had never paid any attention to that particular closet door. Cora shut it behind Mam and me and locked it with a key she took from her jacket pocket.

I had about a million questions, but they would have to wait.

Mam still looked washed out, her forehead pearled with perspiration, her eyes glazed. "Where arf'e?" she mumbled.

"On our way to a doctor," I said, pulling her toward the door outside and the wan light of afternoon.

Five minutes later, I was heading the CR-V down the winding drive, Mam stretched out in the backseat, her head in Aunt Cora's lap. Aunt Cora was trying to use my cell phone to call EMS. But as I rounded the last curve, blue and red lights flashed at the Pinckney gate.

Two sheriff's cruisers were pulled to one side, and the boxy EMS van was parked across the drive, almost blocking Bonnie's rental Toyota from view.

"Oh, no," I said, braking. "Not Bonnie."

"No, not Bonnie," said Aunt Cora. "Augusta."

Then I saw the white Caddy. Its front end was accordioned

against a giant oak tree. The windshield was shattered. And an EMS tech was helping Miss Augusta toward the ambulance's open door, since she'd pushed aside the empty gurney.

"Good news, Mam," I said. "I think we just found you a ride."

Less than ten minutes later, the ambulance, escorted by Will, was speeding toward Charleston, lights flashing. Bonnie and I followed in the CR-V at a slightly slower pace, having been reassured by the EMS tech, who told us Mam was in no real danger. He had already given her an injection of antihistamine, which had made her even groggier but partly restored her color. Will had offered to take one of us with him, and Bonnie and I had to practically push Aunt Cora into the cruiser. Only our contention that Augusta would be more comfortable with her at the hospital made her relent.

"She was pretty funny telling Will to turn off his siren," said Bonnie, who had happened on the accident right before we did.

"She's just afraid someone's going to think she's been arrested," I said.

"But I do think Will wants to talk to her some more. And so do I. You are not going to believe what Marietta told me at the hospital."

"Bet my story's better than yours." I felt all right now that I knew Mam wasn't going to die and that Miss Augusta appeared merely shaken from her run-in with the tree.

"I don't know," Bonnie said. "You've got Mam drinking some tea she was allergic to. My story has bones in it."

"Big deal," I said, glad to see the drawbridge was clear. "Mine's got a ghost."

chapter fifteen

Remember Where You Came From

Aunt Cora was white as a ghost when we found her sitting in the ER waiting room.

"No, Margaret Ann will be fine," she said, seeing our frightened faces. "But Augusta lost consciousness in the ambulance. They don't know if it's a head injury from the accident, some sort of delayed thing, or maybe even a stroke. Pinck and Jamie just got here and were taken straight back." Her face was etched with worry lines. "Did you get hold of J. T.?"

"Yes," Bonnie reassured her. "He was on his way to Georgetown but turned right around. Shouldn't take him too long, if the traffic's not bad on 17. And I left a message with the principal at the high school for Cissy to go on home with Ashley after school and for her to call me from there." Bonnie looked at her watch. "If I haven't heard from her in about thirty minutes, I'll try Ashley's. You sure Mam's going to be okay?"

Aunt Cora nodded. "She's behind those doors. I told the nurse you had all the information—insurance and so forth."

"I guess it's in her wallet," Bonnie said, taking Mam's brown leather shoulder bag from me. "You stay here with Aunt Cora and let me go see what I can find out. About Miss Augusta, too."

I sank into a molded plastic chair next to Aunt Cora. Thanks to her professional dress and manner, Bonnie immediately commanded the attention of the front-desk attendant, as well as all the well males in the vicinity. An orderly looked admiringly in her direction—even as she wobbled slightly in her heels—and the young police officer on duty sat up straighter at his post. He made me think of Will. I wondered where he was. Then I felt guilty for wondering.

"It's not your fault, Lindsey," Bonnie said, coming back and misinterpreting my expression. "Mam really is all right, or soon will be. The nurse said she's asleep right now from that shot they gave her, but we can see her in a bit. There's no way you or she could have known there was something in the tea that would interact with the cold pills she took. I don't care if J. T. is a drug rep, she shouldn't take those samples without a prescription."

"I should have known something was wrong," I said. "The tea tasted weird, which is why I didn't drink it."

"And a good thing you didn't, or you could be in there with Mam. Although maybe not, because you didn't take any cold medicine. Reactions to drug interactions aren't that uncommon, and the FDA doesn't regulate all those herbal supplements. Thank goodness you and Aunt Cora were there."

"What about Augusta?" Aunt Cora asked.

"No news yet," Bonnie said gently. She slumped down next

to me, then frowned in annoyance. "Do you think they could play that television any louder? It seems like you can't go anywhere anymore without a TV blaring. Just try reading in an airport with CNN repeating the same stories over and over again."

"I guess it's supposed to be distracting," I said. "Although this doesn't look like it would take your mind off your troubles."

The wall-mounted TV was tuned to an afternoon soap showing a hospital scene. A handsome doctor with perfectly capped teeth was talking gravely to a woman lying in a bed who appeared to have just had a makeover at the Lancôme counter.

The emergency waiting room wasn't too crowded. A construction worker with outstretched muddy boots and a rag wrapped around one hand was watching the TV with rapt attention. A young, blonde-haired mother in tight blue jeans and an even tighter sweater jiggled a whimpering baby on her knee, the big gold hoops in her ears catching the fluorescent light as she bent her head forward. It made me nervous thinking that any minute the baby was going to yank one of those earrings right off or snatch her baldheaded.

"I still don't get it," I said, looking away. "What was in the tea? Did Miss Augusta try to poison us? And why did she lock us in the attic? It doesn't make sense. We're talking *Miss Augusta*."

We'd gone over some of these same questions on the ride to the hospital, between my telling Bonnie about the secret staircase and her telling me more about Marietta's memories of a graveyard in the woods.

"I don't think she tried to poison you," Bonnie said again. "Didn't you say that Beth gave her the tea? And she drank some, too. Could be that she was starting to react to it when she ran the Caddy into the oak tree."

"She still locked us in. I heard it turn. I thought it was some kind of mistake at first, and we yelled at her. But then Mam started getting sick."

"Maybe locking you in was a mistake, too," Bonnie said. "Maybe she didn't realize she was doing it. Aunt Cora, what do you think?"

"I don't know, dear. Augusta really hasn't been herself the last few weeks. She's seemed distracted, even vague at times, which is not at all like her."

I nodded, remembering Miss Augusta's confusion earlier in the day. "Do you think it's something physical?"

"I don't know," Aunt Cora said. "We all have our senior moments"—she smiled ruefully—"but Augusta has always been sharp as a tack. You get to be our age, though, and you worry about Alzheimer's or a stroke. I know I do, especially after seeing poor Cassie Adams up at the nursing home. Bless her heart, she's fit as a fiddle except she thinks she's a little girl." She sighed. "I've been trying to keep an eye on Augusta, not that it's been easy. You know, Maudie and I call each other every morning, just to make sure everything's all right. But when I suggested something similar to Augusta, she got all huffy, said Marietta gets there early and people are coming through all day. So then I tried calling her in the evenings about different things, but she caught on to that right quick and basically told me to mind my own business." Aunt Cora gave a what-can-you-do shrug. "One night last month, though, I was on my way home from Maudie's, and I thought I'd just swing by. I saw a light in the attic, and that had me worried. I have a key to the downstairs, but Augusta's the only one with a key to the attic that I know of. And she shouldn't be up there by herself at her age."

Apparently, this rule applied only to Miss Augusta and not to our spry aunt, who thought nothing of climbing rickety stairs by flashlight.

"Which is why you became the ghost of Pinckney Plantation," I said. "I told Bonnie about the attic and the door behind the boxes."

"I understand, but I want you girls to promise never to tell anyone else about the secret passageway. Just pretend that I had a key to the third floor and unlocked the door when I heard y'all up there."

"Tell that to Mam," Bonnie said. "She's the one who can't keep a secret. Besides which, isn't it going to look funny that the door is still locked and you, Mam, and Lindsey are all here?"

"You can tell Margaret Ann she must have been dreaming," Aunt Cora said. "And if anybody else asks, I'll tell them I locked the door behind us. I'll say Augusta gave me an attic key for safe-keeping. I was actually thinking of trying to get hold of hers and get a copy made, but then I remembered the staircase. It's been sealed off for years. I imagine there are only a few of us left who ever knew about it in the first place—Augusta, me, Maudie, Marietta. It was locked up even when we were young, probably right after old Colonel Pinckney died."

"Has it always been there?" Bonnie asked. "What was it used for? An escape route from the Yankees?"

Aunt Cora shook her head. "Oh, it might have been, but it was put in when the second house was built, and that was a long time before the War Between the States. Let's see. I think that was during Francis Pinckney's time, but his son was Francis, too. I expect it had more to do with smuggling than anything else—a way to bring in whiskey and sugar and tobacco that he didn't want people to know about or steal. That's why the cage was there."

"You mean it was just a storage locker?" I was disappointed. "What about all those stories? And what about the ghost?"

"Humph," Aunt Cora said. "Lot of foolishness. Of course, Augusta encouraged it by not saying anything. You know, it's practically a requirement that every plantation have a resident ghost. Although I must say the idea came in handy when I started checking on the missing objects. The attic was the first place I wanted to look. I figured if anyone heard any noise up there, they'd be spooked. Poor Cissy. I know I scared her one day. I thought she'd already left."

"Did you find the candlestick in the attic?" I asked.

Aunt Cora looked at me sharply. "No, it needs to be resilvered. Augusta gave it to me because she knew we were taking in that tea set from the historical museum. But I still don't know what happened to the snuffbox or those porcelain figurines. When I asked Augusta about them, she was real vague—something about Bradford having them authenticated. I tell you, I just didn't trust that man. Augusta wouldn't hear a word against him, though. Still, I don't think she would have given him a key to the attic. He must have followed her up there that afternoon. I just wish I'd been there, but I was ferrying some of those historical-society people back to the museum."

"Why didn't you tell us you had an alibi?" Bonnie asked. "Better yet, why didn't you tell Will?"

"I did, dear. That day we had the lemon pie. I told him about going to the gift shop, but that Beth had already gone, so I went ahead and left, too. You didn't seriously think I had anything to do with Bradford's fall, did you? Land's sake, your old aunt might not have liked the man, but that doesn't mean I'd push him down some stairs."

"Maybe Beth did," Bonnie said. "You said she wasn't in the gift shop, though she told us she was. And she sure didn't like him."

"Yes," I said. "It wasn't just that Sue Beth couldn't get married at Pinckney. Bradford took her job, or at least what she thought was her job."

"And she made the tea," Bonnie chimed in. "Maybe she thought Miss Augusta suspected her and was going to finish her off."

"You girls certainly have vivid imaginations," Aunt Cora said. "As far as I know, Augusta still thinks Bradford's death was a dreadful accident. Most people do. Y'all shouldn't be going around making wild accusations, especially about nice women like Beth Chesnut."

I felt chastened, remembering how droopy Beth looked New Year's. But Bonnie wasn't going to back down.

"There are lots of parts of this that don't fit," she said stubbornly. "You've got Miss Augusta acting strange, stuff missing from Pinckney, Bradford dead, Beth being real secretive, what's probably a slave cemetery on Pinckney land that could definitely halt the Magnolia Cay project—"

"A slave cemetery?" Aunt Cora interrupted. "That's the first I've heard about this. Although I wouldn't be at all surprised. There are old grave sites and little cemeteries all over the Low Country."

Bonnie and I filled her in.

"The bone's being tested now," I concluded. "Even though it's just one bone, it would support what Marietta told us. I'm sure Will will want to hear about it."

"What will Will want to hear?"

His brisk entrance into the waiting room was so reassuring that I wanted to burst into tears and fall in his arms. But before I could do or say anything, Aunt Cora asked about Miss Augusta.

"No change," Will said. "I guess they're running tests. I left Pinck filling out a lot of paperwork and Jamie trying to track down his mother."

Aunt Cora sighed, twisting her mottled hands. She looked tired—and old. None of us knew her exact age. Like her lemon pie recipe, it was a secret. It was in the Hill family Bible, but she had that locked away somewhere. Every year on her birthday, August 6, we asked her how old she was. "A lady doesn't tell her age" was all she ever said. I didn't think it was vanity, though, but rather that she didn't want a fuss.

"What were you going to tell me?" Will asked.

I let Bonnie explain. "You'll find that Ray and Pinck's permits to develop Magnolia Cay are on that part of the plantation where Jimmy and Cissy found the bone. Marietta told me today that there was a slave cemetery back there. It's a felony to build on a cemetery. You can move the graves, but it'll cost you a pretty penny, and you have to get the families' permission."

"I'm wondering now if Bradford knew that, too," I said. "All that research of his."

Will nodded. "That's something else we'll be looking into. This whole Magnolia Cay project has caused nothing but trouble from day one. It was already shaping up to be a mess with the water rights and setting aside a wetlands area. A slave cemetery would be an added complication, especially if Bradford was aware of it."

"Jamie might know," Bonnie said. "His name's on the permit application, too. And here he comes now."

Jamie apparently thought we were waiting on news of his great-aunt. "No word yet," he told us. "I'm going down to get Dad some coffee. Can I bring you anything, Miss Cora? How 'bout y'all?"

We shook our heads.

"I'll walk with you," Will said. "Something I want to ask you about."

As they headed down the hall, Aunt Cora sighed again. "I wouldn't want to be in that young man's shoes right now. I figure he and Will are about to have what my daddy used to call a good old-fashioned prayer meeting. And about time."

Bonnie looked at her watch. "I'm going outside and try and call Cissy. I forgot you can't use cell phones in here."

"And I'm going to the rest room," I said.

Aunt Cora pointed me past the reception desk. There were two unisex bathrooms at the end of the hall. And a line. This was why the waiting room wasn't crowded. There were five people ahead of me, one an aged black man in a wheelchair, another a hugely pregnant woman with chipmunk cheeks, a shiny nose, and a resigned expression.

By the time I returned to the waiting room, Bonnie was back, too.

"Thought we were going to have to send out a search party."

"There was a line," I explained. "Cissy?"

"She wanted to have Jimmy carry her up here, but I told her just to stay put, and we'd be along directly," Bonnie reported. "Maybe by the time J. T. gets here, Mam will be awake, and we can all go home."

I sneezed, then sneezed again.

"Goodness, dear, I hope you're not catching something," Aunt Cora said. "This is such a nasty time of year for colds and flu. And no telling what kind of germs are floating around in here." She looked suspiciously at a balding man in a wrinkled business suit sleeping with his mouth open in a chair across the aisle. "Here, I believe I have a clean hankie."

"Thanks, I've got some Kleenex," I said, reaching into my book bag and coming up with a packet of tissues, a movie-ticket stub, a Piggly Wiggly receipt, and the old photo of Pinckney. That was odd. I thought I'd put it back in the envelope. I looked in the cavernous depths, but there was no manila envelope. Curiouser and curiouser, as Alice might say. This whole day had been a down-the-rabbit-hole, through-the-looking-glass kind of experience. Why, we'd even had a tea party.

"What are you doing with that picture?" Aunt Cora asked. "May I see it?"

"We were going to ask you about it," I said, handing it over. "Do you recognize those children? Miss Augusta said she didn't know them."

"She did?" Aunt Cora sounded surprised. "Now I'm really beginning to doubt her mental state. And your sleuthing abilities. Don't you recognize your own grandmother Margaret? I'm not sure who the baby is Margaret's holding—it's such a tiny thing, and that lace is hiding the face—but that toddler is Augusta herself. All those curls. There's a miniature in an oval frame in the downstairs parlor at Pinckney that was probably painted around the same time. When was this taken?"

"It says 1919 on the back," I said.

Cora turned the picture over, then turned it back and studied it again. "That can't be right," she said. "If so, that baby is most likely me." She brought it up close to her face. "Mm. It's hard to tell." She paused, sunk in thought. "This could explain a lot, though."

"How so?" Bonnie asked.

Aunt Cora looked puzzled and a little sad. "Because Augusta and I are the same age," she said. "Her birthday's in May, and mine's in August. We've always laughed about that, how my name should have been Augusta, because of my birthday. She was named after her mother's mother, Augusta Chatham." Aunt Cora stared at the picture, then closed her eyes, remembering. "Seems like your grandmother Margaret told me about this, how the first time she ever saw Augusta was when her parents came to the plantation for Colonel Pinckney's funeral. I was just a baby, and I thought Augusta was, too."

"So you're the baby in the photo," I said. "And that's Augusta, and that's Nanny. We thought she looked familiar. I wonder why Augusta said she didn't recognize anybody."

"Because she didn't want anyone to know how old she is." Aunt Cora caught her bottom lip with her teeth.

"Well, neither do you," I pointed out. "You always say that a lady doesn't tell her age."

"And we're only talking about a year or so," Bonnie added. "I don't see the big deal."

"It's quite a big deal," Aunt Cora said, "if you were born in May 1918 instead of 1919, and your father was overseas with the army until the winter of '18."

Bonnie and I were trying to do the math in our heads.

"You mean . . ."

"That's right," Aunt Cora said. "Augusta is not a Pinckney."

chapter sixteen

Who'd Have Thunk It?

"Pinckney Townsend." The voice rose shrilly from the reception desk. "Do I have to spell it for you?"

Bonnie raised her eyebrows. Aunt Cora pursed her lips. I wanted to put my hands over my ears. Belinda had arrived.

"I am Mrs. Pinck-ney Town-send," Belinda said, emphasizing each syllable. Wearing gray flannel slacks under a long raincoat, she was leaning on the counter with her back to the waiting room, where every head was now turned to watch this diversion. "My husband called to say his aunt, Mrs. Augusta Pinckney Townsend"—she hammered home the name—"was brought in here by ambulance seriously ill. Now, let me ask you again, where are they? I want to be taken to them immediately."

We couldn't hear what the receptionist was saying, but I could see Belinda tapping an Enzo-clad foot impatiently. A Dooney & Bourke purse was slung over one shoulder.

"I have never understood why some people think that being rude will get them further than being nice," Aunt Cora said. "Of course, sometimes you have to be firm, but really, there's no need to cause a scene. Augusta . . ." She faltered, then continued. "Augusta would be appalled at Belinda bandying the Pinckney name around like that." She stood up. "Excuse me, I believe I'll go to the ladies' room."

"Do you think she's all right?" Bonnie asked. We watched Aunt Cora weave her way through the rows of orange chairs and carefully step over the surgical boot of a skinny man in overalls. "Should one of us go with her?"

"No, I think she wants a few minutes to herself. She was worried enough about Mam and Augusta, and now this thing with the picture. And Belinda didn't help."

"Well, that little hissy fit seems to have worked," Bonnie said. Belinda had been pointed down the far hallway toward the closed double doors. "I do like that Burberry coat of hers."

"It would look good on you," I said. "Khaki washes me out."

"They make them in red," Bonnie said. "How many red sweaters did you get this Christmas?"

"Just two. That one I wore New Year's, and the other's not really a sweater. Your mama gave me a red cotton turtleneck from Belk's."

"And your mama sent me a navy blue. What color did Mam get?"

"White, I think. Or yellow. You know them. They probably found a bargain last spring and bought one in every color."

"I wonder what they've found on this trip. Here's hoping it's not straw donkeys. That's what Tom's mother brought me from her cruise last year. She thought it would look good in the family room." Bonnie grimaced. Pottery Barn could have photographed her family room for its catalog. Straw donkeys were not in its pages.

"Where did you put it?"

"Up in the bonus room. Actually, I hung it from the ceiling, and it looked pretty good."

"You said *looked.* What happened?"

"Ben decided it looked like a piñata he saw at some kid in his class's birthday party. So he and Sam beat on it with the broom." She grinned. "Tore that sucker right up."

We looked at each other.

"Do you—"

"—think Miss Augusta killed Bradford?" I finished. "I think Aunt Cora's afraid that she did. And if it is true about her not being a Pinckney, and Bradford somehow found that out and was threatening to tell everybody, she'd have a motive."

"But didn't you say she acted like she'd never seen that picture?"

"*Acted* might be the operative word," I said. " 'And the Oscar goes to Miss Augusta.' " I brushed my bangs from my forehead and rubbed my brow. "You should have seen her when she found out Bradford was dead. We thought she was going to keel over right there."

"Maybe she didn't realize he was dead after he fell down the stairs." Bonnie sat up straighter. She'd gone into her lawyer mode. "Maybe it was an accident, or he threatened her physically. Self-defense."

"So she conked him over the head for good measure?"

Bonnie frowned. "She could have picked up that shell—it was probably right there by the door—to protect herself. She hit out at him, and then he fell."

"But it doesn't change the fact that she left him there, either dead or dying, then turned right around and waltzed back in pretending not to know what was going on. Like I said, 'May I have the envelope, please?' "

Bonnie wasn't going to give up. "She could have gone into a fugue state, disassociated herself so completely she wouldn't remember what happened. Then it all came rushing back to her at once, and she really did almost faint, or whatever."

"Maybe," I said. I didn't want to believe Miss Augusta was a killer any more than Bonnie did. She could be exasperating and imperious, but that was just her way. Good grief, she'd taken over our Girl Scout troop and turned us into plantation tour guides. She'd written our college recommendations. She let us put crab traps in the creek and gave us cuttings from her camellias. She wasn't warm and pillowy like Miss Maudie, but she was as much a fixture in our lives.

"Not guilty by reason of temporary insanity?" I asked hopefully. "How does that work? 'Sorry, Your Honor, I don't remember doing it, but if I did, I must be nuts'?"

"Something like that, but it's more involved." Bonnie sighed. "I'm not a criminal lawyer. Mam probably knows more from watching *Law & Order* reruns. I think anybody who kills anybody has to be a little crazy, or just plain stupid. And the Pinckneys have never been stupid, although some might have been crazy. Wasn't there that great-aunt with the nerves?"

"Lydia," I said. "I remember Nanny talking about her. Cried if anyone looked at her cross-eyed, and would take to her bed at the least excuse. She sleepwalked, too. One night, she sleepwalked outside and right off the dock."

"Did she drown?"

"No, somebody heard her, and they fished her out. Then they packed her off to some private hollerin' house, and she lived there the rest of her life. I'd forgotten all about her." I could hear an approaching siren. "But you're forgetting something, Bonnie. Having somebody crazy in your family isn't going to help if they're not your family."

"I can't imagine Miss Augusta not being a Pinckney," Bonnie said.

"I imagine she can't either."

We sat in silence. I wondered what it would be like to have a literal identity crisis at eighty-something. Denial would be the first reaction. Miss Augusta would have wanted proof. Would she then have killed the messenger?

The siren suddenly cut off. Something was happening at the next bay of doors, out of sight of the waiting room. Real drama occurred there, EMS crews handing off the victims of heart attacks, car wrecks, gunshot wounds, and fires to trauma teams. I wondered how much Mam would remember, and if Miss Augusta had said anything before she collapsed.

My watch said it was almost four. It felt like it should be midnight. I realized I'd never had lunch. I'd been running off caffeine and adrenaline most of the day.

"I'm going to find a snack machine," I said. "Have you had lunch?"

"Barbecue," Bonnie said. She smiled with satisfaction. "But bring me some M&M's—the plain, not the peanut. I'm trying to cut back."

I headed down the hallway, following the sign pointing toward the elevators. Sure enough, several vending machines were lined up across from a bank of pay phones. I put in change and got Bonnie's M&M's. Maybe she'd trade me a few for some of my pretzels. I fed in more quarters. The little bag started to drop, then dangled enticingly, caught behind the plastic. Geez Louise. I should have just followed Bonnie's lead and gone for the chocolate. It was not my day, although at least I wasn't being treated for spiced-tea poisoning. I kicked the machine. The pretzels didn't budge.

"Sorry, miss, but I may have to arrest you for assaulting hospital property. Allow me." Will kicked the machine, and the gold bag obediently fell. He handed me the pretzels.

"Thanks. And who said chivalry was dead?"

I guided a slightly crumpled dollar into the Coke machine's slot, which promptly rejected it. I slid it in again, holding onto it like I was going to try and keep it. "Now, if I can just get this to work."

I offered Will the bag as we walked back to the waiting room.

"Anything new?" he asked, declining the pretzels.

Although they were slightly stale, I was scarfing them down. I used chewing as an excuse not to say anything for a minute. But I was going to have to tell him about the picture and our suspicions. I took a swig of Coke, then started in with the story of the photograph, finishing up with Bonnie's assessment of Miss Augusta's mental state.

"Diminished capacity," he said. "Poor old girl."

"So, do you think she did it?" I asked. "And what about Jamie? How much does he know?"

Will didn't say anything.

I tried again. "I've been thinking about the Caldwells. If Bradford was blackmailing Ray and Pinck about Magnolia Cay, he might also have found something on the Caldwells. You said yourself that it was kind of suspicious having Eddie Smoak guarding collards and old ruins." I was thinking out loud now. "Maybe Miller discovered something valuable about the Hillcrest property. Maybe the Chisholms buried the family silver before the war and forgot where it was. How's that for a motive?"

Will stopped at the entrance to the waiting room. Aunt Cora had rejoined Bonnie. My seat had been taken by a freckle-faced woman holding a dozing toddler.

"Well?" I prodded.

"Lindsey, how many times do I have to tell you I can't discuss an ongoing investigation? Especially now."

"What do you mean, 'Especially now'?"

Will looked at me. "I should have said, 'Especially you.' You know how I feel about you."

"Actually, I don't."

"I thought I made myself pretty clear New Year's Eve."

"And you acted like it never happened last night," I retorted. "Forget the kisses and sweet nothings. Although *nothing* about sums it up. You didn't even say thanks when I told you that stuff about Eddie. Or when you took the shell. How was I supposed to know that you were looking for something like it?"

"That's just the point," Will said. He smoothed his hair back with one hand. "You're not supposed to know. Look where your snooping around has got you. Getting shot at on the dock, Bonnie being run off the road, Mam possibly being poisoned . . ."

"It was an allergic reaction."

"We're still going to test that tea." He stopped. "I shouldn't even have said that. Come on, Lindsey, you're not being fair. You were a reporter." He saw my face. "You *are* a reporter. You know I have to follow procedure. I have a job to do, and there are aspects of it I can't talk about." He pulled his pager from his belt. I thought I saw surprise in his expression as he read whatever number or message was on it. "I have to go. I'll try and call you later at home. Tell the others bye."

He started for the door but stopped and turned back to me when I put my hand on his arm.

"Will," I began.

Oh, what the heck. In front of Bonnie, Aunt Cora, the freckle-faced woman, the entire ER waiting room, and J. T., who was at that moment coming through the sliding glass doors, I stood on the tiptoes of my sneakers and kissed Will on the cheek.

"Be careful," I said. "And you don't have to call. Just come over when you can."

The elevator doors slid closed, and Bonnie and I were alone.

"We're just friends," I said firmly.

"Looked like more than friends to me."

She hit the button for the eighth floor, where Marietta was in the rehab section. Since J. T. was with Mam and Aunt Cora seemed content to leaf through a magazine, Bonnie had decided we ought to go tell Marietta the latest. But I could also see she was dying to interrogate me about that little scene when I'd thrown caution to the wind. What had I been thinking?

"Really," I said. "I was just trying to get him to tell me more about the investigation. You know, making nice—like you with Eddie Smoak."

It was a below-the-belt punch, but she waved it off. "Oh, yeah, right," she said. "That snake. Come on, Lindsey, you can tell me. Mam and I have both seen how moony-eyed you two get around each other."

The elevator stopped at the fifth floor, its doors opening to reveal a beaming young man in a flannel shirt holding a handful of bubble-gum cigars. "Down?" he asked.

"Up," Bonnie said. "And congratulations."

The doors hadn't completely closed before she started in on me again. "Of course, if you don't want to tell me, that's your right, but you know I can keep a secret. I never ratted on you and Mam that time you were supposed to be babysitting me and the two of you sneaked out to go to that party."

"If I remember correctly, we paid you to keep your mouth shut—the babysitting money and all the leftover Halloween candy."

"I didn't say I couldn't be bribed. And y'all are the ones that should feel guilty, leaving a little girl home alone like that."

"You were a twelve-year-old extortionist. Really, Bonnie, Will and I are just friends." The elevator shuddered to a stop. "Really good friends," I added wickedly as I shouldered my way into the press of people crowding to get on. Visiting hours were almost over.

I tapped gently on the half-open door.

Marietta looked up from the muted TV. "Bonnie, what are you doing back here, child? Lindsey, pull that curtain, will you?" She indicated the drape dividing the semiprivate room. "I can't stand having no privacy from perfect strangers traipsing in and out of here all day long. They shout at her 'cause she can't hear a lick."

The elderly occupant of the other bed was sound asleep, her toothless mouth wide open. Her dentures smiled from a glass beside the bed, looking for all the world like those chattering teeth you buy in joke shops. Hospitals are so good at robbing you of your dignity. Marietta looked queenly, though, in a ruby satin-quilted bed jacket over her hospital gown.

"We need to chat with you a minute," Bonnie said. "How are you feeling?"

"Oh, I'm 'bout like I was this morning. Hoped to get a nap this afternoon, but her racket"—she nodded at the curtain—"kept waking me up. Do you have any hand cream in that fancy bag of yours? This hospital air just dries out my skin so. Look how ashy my hands are."

"You keep that," Bonnie said, handing over a small tube I recognized from the last Estée Lauder bonus. Pleasures or Treasures or something like that.

Bonnie signaled me with her eyebrows.

"We came by," I said, "to let you know that Miss Augusta's downstairs having some tests. She had a little accident in the Caddy, but they're taking care of her right now."

"Sweet Jesus! And me stuck here in this bed and can't see to her. What happened? Is she all right?"

"The car hit an oak in the driveway, but she walked to the ambulance," I said. That much was true. Bonnie and I had decided there was no need to upset Marietta with the rest of it until there was more news. But we knew she'd never forgive us if she heard it via the hospital grapevine.

"She drives that car too fast," Marietta said, seemingly satisfied with our explanation. "I done told her over and over again to slow down, we gonna get to heaven 'fore too long, and no need to hurry." She chuckled. "She don't pay me no more mind than she did when my mama was looking after her when she was just a bitty thing."

"Speaking of which," I said, "have you seen this picture before?"

"Oh, yes." Marietta nodded, cradling the photo in her cupped hands. "Don't think Miss Augusta seen it, though. It was just turned in last week for that picture book. I gave it to Beth Chesnut."

"Not to Mr. Bentley?" Bonnie asked.

"Oh, no, what he want it for? He wasn't working on that photo book. Here, you take it back 'fore I get any of that hand cream on it."

"But where did the picture come from?" I asked. "Who brought it by?"

Marietta looked at us, puzzled. "They didn't tell you?"

"They who?" Bonnie asked.

"Why, your mamas. Miss Mary Ann and Miss Boodie."

chapter seventeen

Lights Out, or Two Can Play These Reindeer Games

"I declare," I said. "Looky here, Peaches."

I was sitting on the floor of the hallway at home, a photo album in my lap. It was one of the old-time ones, its soft, crumbling pages the color of graham crackers, the photos carefully pasted in place. A few had slipped over the years and hung crookedly, hiding my grandmother's copperplate captions.

It was obvious where the picture in question had been—the rectangular space was lighter in color than the rest of the page, and you could see the darker honey where the glue had held the corners. And then, of course, there was Nanny's writing: "Margaret and Cora with Augusta Pinckney."

So the evidence of Miss Augusta's age had been here all along, if anyone had bothered to look or make the association. I wondered if Nanny had ever realized it. Probably not. And even if she had, its implication must have escaped her. She'd had enough birthdays to keep up with, what with her own three girls and the sisters and brothers between her and baby Cora.

"No, Peaches, you're not going down there." I grabbed his wiggling hindquarters and pulled him back from the partially opened door leading underneath the house. I'd been in such a rush to look at the picture albums that I hadn't shut it firmly when I'd come in, dropping my jacket and book bag on the floor so as to immediately rummage through the two large shopping bags in which Mama kept the family photos. In case of a hurricane evacuation, they were ready to be put in the trunk of the car, along with the suitcases and Daddy's golf clubs.

Now, Peaches was investigating the depths of the hall closet, his orange brush of a tail sticking out from between Mama's good blue wool coat and an old pink wind suit. She'd have a fit if she found cat hair on that coat. I was going to have to do some serious cleaning before they came home Saturday, or Peaches wouldn't be allowed back.

"Come on, guy, let's get some dinner. Lord, you weigh a ton."

I shut the closet door but left the shopping bags out. I wanted to look through them later and see if there were any other old photos—or missing ones. If Marietta was right that Bradford hadn't seen this picture, how had he known about Miss Augusta's age? Unless there was a duplicate somewhere.

No messages were on the answering machine. Of course, I'd told Will to just come over, brazen hussy that I was turning into. Which reminded me, I better shave my legs.

While Peaches methodically demolished a dish of Science Diet,

I opened a can of Progresso soup, opting for chicken with wild rice over lentil. The lights flickered. I hoped the electricity didn't go off before I could finish fixing my supper. Seemed like every time there was some wind, the power went out on Indigo, especially on the beach. We had a generator for real emergencies, but it was such a pain that we didn't fool with it unless the power company said it was going to be hours—or days, like after Hurricane Hugo—before the trucks and linemen could come from Centerville.

I called Mam's, but Bonnie wasn't there yet. She was taking Aunt Cora to her house on her way to pick up Cissy from Ashley's. J. T. would bring Mam as soon as the doctor released her. We'd ferry Aunt Cora's car from Pinckney tomorrow.

I left a message: "Hey, it's me. I found where the picture was in one of Nanny's albums, so we don't need to go through your mama's. I'm going to eat and probably just go to bed pretty soon. I'm beat. Talk to you in the morning."

The lights flickered again. I'd have to reset every clock in the house. It wasn't even eight yet, but this day had already lasted years. I yawned. At this rate, I was liable to be asleep before Will showed. But he'd wake me up. For sure.

I woke with a start and turned to see what time it was. But there was no orange glow from the digital clock by my bed. I fumbled for the flashlight next to the clock. My watch said ten-thirty. So Will wasn't that late. I smiled and stretched out under the quilt, poking Peaches with my sock-clad foot.

After taking a shower and putting on a pair of corduroys so old they felt like flannel and a long-sleeve Gap T-shirt that was almost as ancient but a flattering shade of pink, I'd climbed on top of the bedclothes with the photo albums to wait for Will. I'd fallen asleep looking at snapshots of Mam, Bonnie, Jack, and me when we were kids. There was a funny one of Mam and me as toddler bathing beauties on the beach, Mam with her face scrunched up like someone—probably me—had swiped her sand bucket. The best picture, though, was of the three of us girls on Nanny's glider. Six-year-old Mam was sitting in the middle with her arms draped over Bonnie and me, the camera apparently catching her in midsentence. Typical. Bonnie looked more like the Sunbeam Bread girl than ever, blonde curls on top of her head. She and Mam were wearing matching sailor-girl outfits. I had on a pink sleeveless shirt, and a damp fringe of bangs stuck to my forehead. Typical.

It sure was taking Will awhile to ring the doorbell. I was certain I'd heard him pull into the driveway. I crawled across the bed to look out the window, leaning on the sill. The full moon made it look practically like day outside. Yep, the power was off, at least on this stretch of beach. The Hendersons next door were weekenders only, but there were no lights across the street at the Godwins'.

And no sheriff's cruiser in my driveway.

But there was someone under the house. I couldn't see them, but the beam of a strong flashlight shone on the driveway as I looked down, pressing my nose to the cold pane of glass.

I sucked in my breath. The light moved, so I could no longer see it. Had I locked the hall door? I remembered shutting it after hauling Peaches back in, but as for turning the deadbolt . . .

Coward that I am, I wasn't about to go see if it was locked. The portable phone wouldn't be working, so I crawled across the bed to find my cell, then back toward the window, scrunching down in the space between the bed and the wall. Let's hope I could get a signal.

"Matthews residence."

"Bonnie," I whispered. "Sorry, I meant to call Will."

"Well, excuse me for answering. I'll hang up so you can dial the right number."

"Wait, don't go," I implored.

"Why are you whispering?"

"Because there's someone under the house, and the electricity's off, and I think I forgot to lock the hall door."

"It's probably raccoons."

"With a flashlight?"

"Why didn't you say so? Where are you?"

"In my room, hiding by the bed. Just a sec." I strained to listen. "Bonnie, I didn't lock the door. Someone just opened it."

Peaches had heard the door, too. His ears pricked with interest. I shrank closer to the floor.

"Lindsey, stay where you are. Don't hang up. And don't panic. I'll go get my cell and call dispatch. Be right back."

I heard her put the phone down. But I also heard someone moving downstairs.

So did Peaches. He leaped off the bed and padded across the room and into the hall leading to the stairs.

I hesitated. Should I go after him? Whoever was downstairs probably thought no one was home. Peaches might make them think otherwise. But cats stay home by themselves all the time. I should stay put and remain calm.

But what if the intruder came up here? There was no room to crawl under the bed, thanks to the Fox pack-rat genes. I'd switched off the flashlight upon hearing the door open downstairs, but the moonlight made the room bright. Daddy's old nine-iron was leaning by the closet door, right where I'd left it the other night. I eased out of my hiding place, put the cell phone on the pillow, and tiptoed gingerly toward the closet.

Just holding the golf club made me feel better. If anyone came in the door, I'd bash them over the head. Right. My stomach did a flip-flop. What if there were more than one? What if it was a ring of thieves hitting unoccupied beach houses? What if it was a home invasion? What if it was a psycho killer who hated cats and writers?

There was a crash downstairs, followed by a yowl.

Peaches!

Thank goodness the hall and stairs were carpeted, or I might have broken my neck. My socks slipped only once. I banged up against the right stair wall, holding the golf club in front of me like a lance. It hit the framed family pictures marching up the left wall, knocking down the portrait of Mam in her wedding gown with Bonnie and me on either side in those wretched velvet dresses. Whose bright idea was it that we should wear our hair up, anyway?

I skidded to a stop at the bottom of the stairs. There was no one in the living room, but the front door was wide open, and I could see a dark figure running down our boardwalk toward the dunes and the beach. Peaches was in hot pursuit.

Great. A declawed, indoor fur ball that slept around the clock had suddenly decided to become an attack cat. The burglar must be wearing eau de tuna or carrying off a turkey. But I had to get Peaches. This wasn't his home; he might never find his way back.

It was freezing. My socks didn't do so well on the wooden steps, and I lost all sensation in my feet by the time I sank into the sand of the dune path. I used the golf club like a ski pole to help get up the hill. Thank goodness for the moon.

Peaches had slowed, no doubt trying to figure out this giant litter box he had ventured into.

"Here, kitty," I called. "Peaches, come here."

He veered into a clump of sea oats and disappeared.

"Peaches!" I was gasping as I reached the crest of the dune. If I could just grab him and run back to the house . . .

"Gotcha!"

But no. His tail brushed my hand as he scooted past me toward the beach. Oh, Lord, cat, I thought. Please, please. He hopped over a large piece of driftwood. My foot caught in the dollar weed twining in the sandy dune.

The beach stretched like a white sheet beneath the star-strewn sky. The tide was coming in, the waves unfurling fifty yards away. Peaches headed straight toward them—or maybe toward the hooded person silhouetted at ocean's edge, who at that very moment was heaving something into the water.

What the . . . ?

I heard a splash. Then he—burglar? killer? idiot?—started wading into the water. Was I watching a suicide? Peaches appeared as mystified as I was, having stopped a few feet from the waves. He sat and began nonchalantly washing one paw.

Maybe we could still get out of this mess undetected. I'd discarded the golf club at the top of the dune during my unsuccessful grab-the-cat routine. I hoped I wouldn't need it.

Peaches rolled over on his back. He knew I wanted to pick him up, and he wasn't going to make it easy.

There. I'd just started to straighten up with an armful of damp, sandy cat when there was more splashing. Peaches used my chest as a launching pad to spring to freedom. Something hit me from the side, and I went down on my knees. Then someone was on top of me, pushing my head into the sand.

I bucked like a horse. The attacker fell away, and I saw his face for the first time.

I screamed.

He wasn't human. Or at least his features weren't. They looked like melted candle wax. Then I realized he was wearing a pantyhose mask.

He lunged for me and caught my right ankle as I tried to scramble to my feet. I was on my back now, being pulled across the sand toward the water. Shells scraped my back.

"Let me go!"

I squirmed and kicked with my other foot, grazing his shoulder. He stumbled but maintained an iron grip on my ankle, dragging me closer to the water. I took a deep breath, and this time when I kicked, I put my whole body into it. He went down, falling into the water. My sock went with him.

I dug my elbows into the sand and hoisted myself to a sitting position, struggling to stand. But the attacker wasn't through. This time, he had a large shell in his hand—shades of Bradford Bentley. He thrashed through the water toward me.

The shell hit my forearm. It hurt like the devil. At least it wasn't my forehead. I shoved back. Two could play this reindeer game. If I could just stand up . . .

I wasn't prepared for the tackle. My face was in the water. A wave broke over my head. Then the attacker was on me again, pushing me farther under.

I bucked like I had before, but no go. I got my face far enough out of the water to take a deep breath, then plunged into an oncoming wave, taking us both into deeper water. I knew this beach, and I knew by the colder water that this was right where the sand bar dropped off. One minute you were wading ankle deep, and the next you were in over your head.

The move surprised him. And either he wasn't a good swimmer or his padded parka was weighing him down. He was still on my back, but now I was his flotation device. He wanted to climb me like a tree. My lungs felt like they were going to burst.

Now or never. I went completely limp and forced myself downward. I slipped from his grasp and came up for air a few feet away. I hadn't been a lifeguard for nothing. I immediately started treading water, the current tugging at me, wanting to carry me out to sea. I struck out parallel to the shore, using a combination crawl and sidestroke to keep the now-floundering man in view.

He went under, then popped up farther out, one arm waving. Was he genuinely in distress, or was this a ruse?

"Swim sideways, not forward!" I shouted.

He went down again.

No, I wasn't going to give him another chance to drown me. But I couldn't let him die, could I?

I was about to dive and see if I could come at him from behind, get him in a headlock, and tow him to safety, but a large wave took the decision out of my hands. As I felt the wave rise beneath me, I body-surfed with the flow, letting it lift me onto the sand bar. The masked man had a rougher time of it. The same wave tumbled him into the shallows. He made it to all fours, his head hanging, coughing up water and who knew what else. Disgusting.

My teeth were chattering. The night air was colder than the water. I scraped the hair off my face and rubbed my eyes, unsure if the salt was tears or ocean. We'd come ashore in front of the Hendersons'. I recognized the small gazebo that marked the path to their house. Good. It wasn't far back to our dune. I was starting to feel like a Popsicle.

"Lindsey!" Bonnie's voice came out of the darkness. Then a beam of light scanned the beach. "Lindsey!"

"Over here!" I called. I waved and started limping toward her. Help had arrived.

But I turned my back too soon. Drowning Guy suddenly regained enough strength to shove me down with one hand as he ran past, heading for the Hendersons'.

"Bonnie!" I yelled. "Get him!"

She might look like a duck when she ran, but she was fast. She tackled him right in front of the gazebo and was straddling his back by the time I reached them.

"Move and I'll bust your head with this flashlight." She looked at me. "Are you all right? Olivia ought to be here any sec."

I nodded, too give out to say anything for the moment.

"Who is this bozo? And what's with this?" She poked at the back of his head, where the parka hood had fallen away to reveal wet brown nylon.

"Pantyhose," I said. I reached down and yanked the soggy mess off his head.

"Oh, my word!" Bonnie exclaimed.

I looked at my attacker in astonishment. Dark roots were showing.

I always knew Pen Upchurch was a bottle blonde.

"Dad-gum," Bonnie said. "Mam is not going to believe she missed this."

chapter eighteen

Well, I Declare!

"I can't believe I missed all this!" Mam said. She smeared some grape jelly on another piece of wheat toast and waved the knife at me. "You really didn't know it was Pen until you got the mask off?"

"No, I thought it was a guy," I said, looking away from the breakfast remains on Mam's kitchen table. She'd recovered completely from her adverse reaction to the tea, although her nose sounded stuffed up. She'd been in bed asleep by the time Bonnie brought me and Peaches home with her. Because the power was still off, there was no heat at my parents' house, so it made sense to camp out on Mam's couch again. I'd slept right through J. T. heading off to work and Cissy to school. So had Bonnie.

"But Pen's short and small," Mam insisted. "How could you think she was a man?"

"Because I'm short, too. Because it was dark, and I was lying on the beach with her looming over me," I said. "And she may be small, but she's strong. She must work out."

I shuddered at the memory of our wrestling match, then wished I hadn't. I ached all over, and my arms were scratched and bruised.

"That one's about the color of this jelly," Mam observed, pointing at a bruise on my forearm.

"That's where she got me with the shell," I said.

"Stupid woman," Bonnie said. "I still can't believe she thought Uncle Lee's ashtray was the shell she used to hit Bradford. And throwing it in the ocean with the tide coming in—of course, it's going to wash right back in."

"What do you expect? She's from off," I said. "One big white shell looks just like another to her. Daddy's was right there in the living room. Mama's been using it as a doorstop since he quit smoking."

We had already figured out that Pen was looking for the shell in my car. When it wasn't there, she searched for a way into the house. I'd made it easy for her.

"She's still stupid," Bonnie said. "You should have heard her sniveling to Olivia that Lindsey attacked her. But then Olivia held up that pantyhose mask, and she started bawling."

"Were they No Nonsense or something more sheer?" Mam asked. "Maybe L'Eggs Silken Mist? I like those."

"Honestly, Mam, I wasn't paying much attention to the brand of pantyhose." I took a sip of Coke. "I had a few other things on my mind, like trying not to get killed."

"They were pretty sheer, I think," said Bonnie. "It's hard to tell when they're wet. But I know they weren't control-top because they didn't have that heavy part at the top."

"Probably sheer toe to waist then," Mam affirmed. "Pen wouldn't need control-top."

At this rate, it was going to take all morning for Bonnie and me to catch Mam up on all she'd missed. We had started at breakfast—Coke and toast for me; bacon and eggs and a lot of coffee for Bonnie—with the revelations about the slave cemetery and the questionable circumstances surrounding Miss Augusta's birth. "My stars!" Mam had said. "Miss Augusta not a Pinckney? Now I've heard everything."

But she hadn't, mostly because she kept going off on tangents. Had we noticed how cute the intern was at the hospital? Had we met her nurse, Trixie? Did we think her weird dream about going down into a hole following a bright light was one of those near-death experiences? No, I'd said quickly. She hadn't been anywhere near death. Bonnie added that some drugs had hallucinogenic side effects. "Maybe that was it," Mam had agreed.

"Pen caved pretty quick, once Olivia got those handcuffs on her," I said now. "She started off saying she was just helping Miss Augusta, that she'd seen her push Bradford down the stairs and hit him over the head, and how she took the shell to protect her."

"Blackmail her is more like it," Bonnie said.

"You should have heard Bonnie," I told Mam. "She was great. She told Pen to tell it to her lawyer, because no one was going to take her word over a Pinckney's."

"That's when she started crying and cussing the Pinckneys every which way to Sunday," Bonnie continued. "Good thing you weren't there to hear that, Mam."

"I wish I had been there," Mam said. "I'd have wanted to punch her lights out. Imagine trying to blame Miss Augusta, and her lying there in a coma and not able to defend herself."

"Well, Pen didn't know that," Bonnie pointed out. "Good thing, too, or she might have shut up then and there. But no, she just kept ranting away, saying it was all the Pinckneys' fault, that Bradford had this big crush on Julia when he was a freshman. 'Julia Pinckney this, Julia Pinckney that.' Then she said if it wasn't for the Pinckneys, Bradford would never have come to Indigo and met up with Kit again."

"Again?" Mam said. "I thought Kit was Pen's friend from college. Oh, don't tell me, you mean Kit and Bradford really were having an affair? How come you didn't tell me this before?"

"Because you were too busy talking Nurse Trixie and pantyhose," I said. "Apparently, from what Pen said, Bradford and Kit were going at it like rabbits whenever they got the chance. And supposedly, it wasn't the first time, although Pen didn't know that until she came down here. I guess she cottoned onto something, which was why she went up in the attic that day. She followed Bradford, thinking he was going to meet Kit, when probably he was looking for Miss Augusta or just snooping around. Of course, he could have been looking for a new love nest."

Pen had broken down sobbing during the arrest, hiccuping about what a lying, cheating son of a bitch Bradford was, and how Kit was no better, maybe worse. If the woman hadn't just tried to drown me, I might have felt sorry for her. As it was, I'd watched her collapse in the backseat of Olivia's cruiser with relief, burying my face in Peaches' sandy fur. He'd appeared from under the house as Olivia force-marched Pen up from the beach. "Crazy cat," I'd muttered, scooping him up.

Now, he was sleeping on Mam's window seat in the early-morning sunlight, having dined royally on some tuna, since I'd forgotten to bring his Science Diet. His litter box, too. I'd made a makeshift one in the laundry room out of a box and some shredded newspaper for the time being. His one set-to with Chloe had ended when Peaches batted her across the nose and Chloe fled to the den for safety.

"So, jealousy was the motive all along," Mam mused. "Who'd have thunk it? She was still carrying a torch for him. I bet she can plea-bargain it down to manslaughter, or maybe claim self-defense. That happens all the time on *Law & Order*."

"We still don't know if Miss Augusta was in the attic, too," Bonnie said. "And we might not know until she wakes up."

We were all silent for a moment. There was a chance Miss Augusta wouldn't wake up. The doctors had told Pinck as much last night, Mam had reported. When she'd called this morning, there'd been no change. Mam had then called Aunt Cora, who told her she and Miss Maudie were already starting a prayer chain.

"Miss Augusta could have been the one to push Bradford, like Pen claims," Bonnie said, frowning. "I still think he was blackmailing her, from everything Aunt Cora said. That would explain why some stuff is missing. People always think the Pinckneys are rich, but Miss Augusta's practically put her last dime into the plantation. She might have sold or given Bradford a few antiques, like candlesticks and that snuffbox. And it had to be something other than the slave cemetery, because she's already thinking how to turn that to Pinckney's advantage. It has to be the age thing. He must have found out about her real birthday when he was researching the book. Only where's the evidence?"

"Maybe it's on the computer disk Mam gave Pen," I said. Mam glared at me. "Okay, the disk *we* gave her. But wasn't there supposed to be more than one? What happened to that box of pictures and stuff?"

"You used the box for Peaches," Mam said. "But here's everything that was in it. Cissy and I just scooped up what was on top of the desk at Pinckney."

She picked up a stack of pictures and envelopes on the kitchen counter and began spreading them out on the table. Bonnie hurriedly moved the last of the dishes to the sink. I put the jelly jar in the fridge.

Mam sorted through the pictures. Bonnie shook out envelopes. I picked up an old, coverless copy of *Charleston Receipts* and began flipping back to front through pages brown with age. Someone had penciled checkmarks by favorite recipes, including Iced Green Tomato Pickles. It was too early in the day for pickles, not to mention Mrs. Alston Pringle's Calf's Head Soup.

"Hey, have y'all ever heard of Cassina Tea?" I asked. I read from the book: " 'This is one of the most delicious native drinks and compares favorably with most imported teas if brewed properly.' In the spring, you strip the young green leaves from the cassina—or Christmas berry—bush, and then you toast them in a hot oven 'until they are brown and crisp enough to crumble in the hand.' Maybe Beth made Cassina Tea."

"You can ask her later," Mam said absently. "She's supposed to come over this morning and get these pictures. Now, who do you suppose this is?" She displayed a color snapshot of a teenage girl with a strawberry-blonde bouffant, wearing what looked like a green prom dress. "She might be one of the Gateses. They all have lots of freckles. Why don't people put names—"

"Here it is!" Bonnie held up the disk in triumph. "It was in this envelope that stuck back together, so it looked like it hadn't been opened. Is the computer working?"

"It better be," Mam said.

It was. Bonnie and I huddled over Mam's shoulder.

"Which file should I open first?" she asked. "There could be something in any of these—Indigo, Pinckney, Manigault. I wonder if there's something about the slave cemetery there."

"We can come back to it," I said. "Open the Chatham file. That's Miss Augusta's family in Richmond."

" 'The Chathams are a distinguished Virginia family whose roots were firmly planted in the colonial era,' " Bonnie read aloud. "Blah, blah, blah. Where's the good stuff?" She leaned over and hit the scroll key.

"Hey!" Mam said. "I was reading."

"Stop!" I said. "Look, there. 'Senator Robert Chatham's daughter Edith grew into a strong-willed young woman whose aristocratic features were crowned with glorious red curls.' Geez, Bradford's prose is pretty purple."

"Pinckney purple," Bonnie giggled. She picked up where I'd left off. " 'Although Edith had many suitors among the students at the nearby universities, as well as her father's aide, William Bowen, she was attracted to a handsome Southern soldier. Major Henry Pinckney, an officer and a gentleman whose father owned a fine plantation on Indigo Island in South Carolina, had recently returned from service in France when he met Edith at a ball in the nation's capital. Edith was said to have left a trail of broken hearts in her wake when she eloped with Major Pinckney, but the senator gave the union his blessing. Edith and Henry named their first child Augusta, after Edith's late mother, and planned to name their first son Robert, but it was not to be. Edith succumbed to pneumonia not long after the couple and their daughter returned from a sad journey to Indigo Island in 1919 to attend the funeral of Henry's father. The grief-stricken young husband, by now a colonel, thereafter devoted himself to his army career but always made sure young Augusta was well looked after, first by Senator Chatham's niece, Elizabeth, and later by his own sister Letitia.' "

"Oh, pooh," Mam said. "That doesn't prove anything. He doesn't have any dates for when Augusta was born."

"But he's got footnotes. Look for number three, Bonnie."

She read the sources: " 'Chatham family letters, Bible, and records, U.S. Army records. Photographs from this period include Edith Chatham with her father at her debut, 1916; Maj. Henry Pinckney in the spring of 1918; undated photograph of Augusta Pinckney at Pinckney Plantation with two unidentified children.' "

"Nanny and Aunt Cora," Mam said.

"So there was another photograph," I said. "Bradford must have found it, and since he knew when Colonel Pinckney died, he figured out the rest from his research. He's probably got his photo in a safe-deposit box somewhere."

"But who was Augusta's father?" Bonnie asked.

"We may never know, unless Bradford dug that up, too. He's written this part of the book so that if you read between the lines, you can maybe get some idea. Edith and her 'trail of broken hearts,' etc. And he took the trouble to mention her father's aide. I bet he knew more on William Bowen. But it's all very ambiguous."

"Edith could have been seduced by this Bowen guy, and he was already married," Bonnie said. "Or if she was in Washington with her father, think of all the sleazy political types who might have taken advantage of her, trying to win her father's favor. You can't tell me things back then were that different from now."

"Or maybe she fell in love with an unknown soldier who was killed in battle," Mam said. "He might never have known he was going to be a father. Bradford's book sure reads like a bad romance."

"And it's for sure Miss Augusta wouldn't have wanted it

published." I wondered how Henry Colleton would handle this information, or if the book project would be put on indefinite hold.

"We'll need to hand this disk over to Will," Bonnie said. "It might be evidence they'll need if there's a trial, or maybe they could use it as leverage with Pen, to see what else she knows. I'm sort of surprised we haven't heard from him. Or rather, dear cousin"—she looked at me—" I'm surprised *you* haven't heard from him."

"You know as much as I do," I said airily.

"You were trying to call him when you got me instead."

"I was in fear of my life," I said. "He's the sheriff. He's got a gun."

"Sure he does." She started batting her eyes and doing her Southern belle act. " 'Oh, Will, you handsome devil, you. Why don't you come on over and show me your gun?' "

"Quit," I said. "You are being just plain evil."

"What are you two going on about?" Mam asked, intent on the computer screen.

"It's nothing," I said. I shoved Bonnie with my hip. Miss Graceful promptly fell against the back of the chair and onto the carpet, pulling me down with her.

"Look out, you two!" Mam swiveled around in the chair. "I declare, y'all are like a couple of kids."

The doorbell rang. Mam was only too happy to step over us to go answer it.

"Hey, Beth," I heard her say. "Come on in. The others are back in the study, laughing like hyenas. You want some coffee?"

"Maybe she'd rather have tea," I whispered to Bonnie.

"Stop, Lindsey. Help me up. We better go make nice."

"Should we tell Beth about the disk and everything?"

"Not yet," Bonnie said. "Which means we better hightail it into the kitchen before Mam spills all."

But it was Beth talking nineteen to the dozen as we entered the room.

"When I first heard, I couldn't believe it, I tell you what. It was a shock. Just imagine. Right here on Indigo under our noses. And Marietta! That's probably why she was run over, don't you know. She's lucky she's not dead. Good thing they have all that security at the hospital now or they might have tried again. Maybe they did, for all we know, and that's why they had the raid last night."

"What raid?" Bonnie asked.

Mam had her mouth open to answer, but Beth was there first. "At the Caldwells'," she said. "It's like something on TV, one of those crime shows, not that I ever watch them, but I know some people do. That's what I told Martha Bridwell when she told me. She lives out that way, y'know. Saw the flashing lights and everything, just like on TV. I don't think there were any shots fired, though. Leastways, she didn't say so. She made Ted get up and go find out what was going on. Mind if I help myself to some coffee?"

"Here, let me get it for you." I reached for a mug. Mam was standing there like a bump on a log, her mouth open. "And would you mind going back to what you were saying about a raid at the Caldwells'?"

"Oh, no, I don't mind at all," Beth said. "I was just telling Margaret Ann. The FBI raided the Caldwells' farm last night. They arrested Miller on federal slavery charges. Do y'all have any Sweet 'n Low?"

chapter nineteen

A Name by Any Other Name

"Slavery?" Mam had recovered her voice. "That's impossible. There are no slaves on Indigo. Haven't been since the Civil War. Will Equal do?"

"Migrant workers," Beth said. "Equal's fine, thank you. Apparently, Miller and that fellow he's partnered with in south Florida have been keeping some of the workers locked up like prisoners. Take their passports or green cards or whatever—I think a lot of the Haitians might be illegals to start with—and then charge them for food, housing, transportation, whatever. And by the time they finish, there's not one red cent left over for those poor people to send their families."

"Well, I never!" Mam exclaimed.

Bonnie nodded. "It's not just farm workers. There was a case up in New York, I think, where a factory owner was arrested for doing something similar to these young girls from Mexico. They were working as seamstresses eighteen hours a day and living about eighteen to an apartment. Only way they found out about it was when some of the girls ran away and were arrested as prostitutes."

"How did they find out about this?" I asked. It was hard to take in. Miller Caldwell a slaver! My mind jumped to Luis. Was he involved, too? "What about Luis Rivera? And did you say something about Marietta?"

"Now, that's the part I was telling Margaret Ann," Beth said. "I guess I got ahead of myself. Marietta's the one who found out. Did you know her nephew put his house on that lot bordering the Caldwells' near Hillcrest?" She looked at us expectantly.

"We saw it Monday," Mam said. She was playing with the wooden salt and pepper shakers, just itching for Beth to finish her story so she could tell ours. I wasn't sure who held the trump card—Beth with Miller keeping migrant workers as slaves, or Margaret Ann with Pen beaning Bradford.

"Marietta was out there babysitting, oh, let's see, must have been several months ago, right after he first moved in." Beth leaned forward and lowered her voice. "It was nighttime, and she heard all this crying and wailing coming from the back of the property. She thought at first it was ghosts, but she got her a flashlight and went to investigate. And she found some of the workers locked up in one of those little shacks. There were bars on the windows."

Beth stopped long enough to take a sip of coffee. Mam started to say something, but Beth beat her to it. "They didn't speak much English, but I guess Marietta understood enough of that Haitian Creole—it's supposed to be a lot like Gullah—to figure out something was wrong. I think she probably would have marched right up to Miller and given him what for, but the workers told her they'd be killed, and she might be, too. And look what happened!"

"So she did tell somebody." Mam was ready for the pause this time.

"You bet she did. She told Henry Colleton. He's kin to her, too, you know. Although come to think of it, I don't know why she didn't tell Olivia. She's her grand-niece and a deputy sheriff, and Henry's just a cousin. Maybe she was scared for Olivia, her being here on Indigo and a woman. Marietta can be kind of old-fashioned. Her and Miss Augusta both—"

I thought Mam was going to have a conniption if Beth didn't hurry up. "Beth," she interrupted. "What happened next?"

"Oh, Henry contacted the FBI, and they met with him and Marietta and said they had an ongoing investigation and didn't want to jeopardize it. So they swore them to secrecy, and they even made Marietta—what do you call it?—a confidential informant."

"Yes, a C.I.," Mam said quickly. "Go on."

"Well, that's it," Beth said. "Marietta went hunting haints and found Haitians." She held out her mug to me. "Maybe just half a cup?"

"What about the raid?" Bonnie asked, pushing another packet of Equal across the table.

"They had it," Beth said. "Coordinated it with the authorities in Florida. They took the workers to someplace in Charleston to meet the immigration people. And they carted Miller off—I guess to jail—along with one of those Smoaks they think ran down Marietta. I don't know about Kit yet. I called out to the house this morning and just got the answering machine. Bless her heart, I'm sure she had no idea that Miller—"

I cut her off. "What about Luis? Was he arrested?"

"Oh, no," Beth said. "Didn't I tell you that? He headed up the whole raid. He's an undercover FBI agent."

"Mercy!" Mam said. "I thought they were only that good-looking on TV. Lindsey, where are you going?"

I zipped up the red windbreaker I'd picked off the peg by the back door. It was an old one of Daddy's I'd grabbed last night. My keys were in the den. "I'll be back in just a bit," I called over my shoulder.

"But where are you going?" Mam repeated. "And what should we tell Will if he calls?"

"Tell him I've gone to see a man about a dog."

The road to Hillcrest was deserted, the shoulder—or what there was of it—rimed with frost where sunlight had yet to penetrate the deep shade of the evergreens. Smoke rose from the chimney of one small house, whose unseen occupants had yet to take down their Christmas decorations. The red nose of their forlorn plastic reindeer had long ago faded to pink.

I was trying not to drive too fast, worried that there might be patches of black ice. The last thing we needed was another trip to the ER.

A sheriff's cruiser was parked sideways at the turnoff to Hillcrest, barring entrance.

"Good morning, ma'am," the young deputy said. The rectangular brass nameplate on his khaki uniform was almost hidden behind the open black padded jacket. *H. Gates*. I didn't know him, but the red hair and freckles were a dead giveaway. Centerville was full of Gateses. "The road is closed this morning. Can I help you with something?" He looked at me closely. "Ma'am, are you hurt? Did somebody hit you? Your husband? Your boyfriend?"

"No, no," I reassured him. "I'm fine. This"—I indicated the bruise on my cheekbone—"happened last night. And y'all have the person who did it. I'm Lindsey Fox. Is Major McLeod here?"

"No, ma'am," Deputy Gates said. "He's up in Centerville with the sheriff. I could call in and get a message to him."

"No, that's all right," I said. Of course Will was tied up, what with Pen and this Hillcrest thing. Otherwise, he would have called. "Actually, I'm here to see Agent Rivera."

Calling Luis by his title seemed to reassure the deputy I wasn't a stranger to the situation. I wondered what the *H.* stood for. Harry? Harvey? Hank?

"I'm not supposed to let anyone by without credentials," he said. He looked apologetic. Then his brow cleared. "There's Agent Rivera now."

A dark green Explorer pulled up on the side of the road. The dog was in the backseat, his nose pressed against the window, his plume of a tail waving like a flag. He obviously wanted to get out with Luis but reluctantly stayed put.

"Lindsey!" Luis said. "I tried to call your house, but here you are. You know what's happened?"

"It's a small island," I reminded him.

We were standing in the middle of the road. Luis looked at Deputy Gates, who suddenly seemed to remember something he had left in his car.

"Yes," he said. "I heard about your adventure last night. Are you all right? That bruise . . ."

"It looks worse than it is," I said. "Deputy Gates was ready to call out the law on my abusive boyfriend, but I told him it was already taken care of."

"Yes, it appears so, although I haven't heard any details."

"Me neither," I said. "I don't think Indigo has seen this much excitement since the DEA swooped in a few years back and rounded up some deep-sea charters that were hauling in more than fish." I stopped. "You're leaving, aren't you?"

"I have to. That's why I called. I'll be in Charleston a couple of days, but after that, I'm not sure."

"I understand good farm managers have their pick of jobs these days."

He had the good grace to look sheepish. I could almost bet Luis Rivera wasn't his real name, just another part of his FBI cover.

"I would have told you if I could," he said. "The funny thing is, I liked being here. And I was pretty good at running the place, even if I say so myself." He looked out over the brown stubble of half-frozen fields.

"What'll happen to it now?"

"I don't know." He sighed. "It's out of my hands. The big guns and the lawyers will get into it. It'll probably be months before there's a trial, if it comes to that. The Florida operation is even bigger, with a lot more workers and money involved. Compared to it, the Caldwells' Indigo farm is pretty small potatoes."

"Or tomatoes."

"Yes, tomatoes." Luis smiled, then looked serious. "I'll miss those tomatoes. And I'll miss you, Lindsey Fox. I hoped to get to know you better. Maybe once I get wherever . . ."

"I'll take the dog," I said.

"You will? Are you sure?"

"Yes," I said. "I'm sure. That is, if he still needs a home."

"He does." We both looked at Pablo, who hadn't taken his eyes off us. His mouth was open, as if he were smiling. "He's a good dog. I'd keep him if I could. I didn't expect for things here to be wrapped up so quickly. I was going to put him in a kennel while I figured out what to do with him."

"Can I take him now? Will he go with me?"

"Sure," Luis said. He smiled again. "He probably won't even miss me. He likes the women, this one. He already thinks you're the cat's pajamas."

Peaches the cat did not take kindly to Pablo the dog. He immediately puffed up when the dog loped into Margaret Ann's den. He hissed twice, spit once, and leaped on the back of the sofa to watch in disdain as Chloe discovered she had a new best friend. The two dogs were now frisking around the backyard, Pablo lifting his leg at every bush, marking the territory.

"I'm going to call him Doc," I told Mam. We were sitting on the back steps, which had been warmed by the sun. Bonnie was upstairs packing.

"Is that his name?" Mam asked.

"No. He's been P-a-b-l-o." I spelled it out.

"Pablo!" Mam stretched out the *a* so it sounded like *pablum*, but the dog nevertheless pricked up his ears and looked at us.

"Shh," I said. "Doc! Come, here, Doc."

He galumphed over, licked my hand, and then wandered to inspect the Confederate rose Mam was trying to grow from a cutting from Pinckney. He lifted his leg again.

"Why Doc?" Mam asked.

"Remember my big yellow stuffed dog, the one Daddy's friend the doctor gave me when I was a baby?"

"The Doc you slept with every night until he practically fell apart? Aunt Mary Ann had to slipcover him because his stuffing was leaking everywhere."

"She did a good job. We didn't cover his head because that

would have changed his personality."

Margaret Ann rolled her eyes. "You had so many stuffed animals that there wasn't room in the bed for me when I came to spend the night."

"But Doc was my favorite. He went to college with me."

"And where is he now? Did he graduate?"

"To the top of my closet, in a pillowcase. His stuffing started coming out again."

"So now you have a real Doc. But what's wrong with Pedro?"

"Pablo," I whispered. "Pablo Fox sounds like a cartoon character, or the president of Mexico."

"Doc Fox sounds like something out of Uncle Remus. You can't just go changing a dog's name." Mam sounded adamant.

"People change their names all the time," I pointed out. "You changed yours when you got married."

"That's different," she said. "It was my last name. You don't go changing first names."

"Oh, come on. What about Minnie Dean Barksdale? She went off to college and became Mindy. Half the people in our family don't go by their given names, you included."

The back door opened. "What are y'all talking about?" Bonnie sat next to Mam. "Slide over some."

"Names," I said. "I'm changing the dog's name to Doc."

"After your stuffed dog," Bonnie said. "That's sweet."

"See?" I elbowed Mam in the ribs.

"I just think it might confuse him, getting a new owner and a new name. But you're right. Our family has some real doozies, when it comes to names. Just look at our mamas and Aunt Rae."

"Yeah," Bonnie said. "What was Nanny thinking? Fairy Rae, Mary Annette, and Beulah Elizabeth. No wonder they became Rae, Mary Ann, and Boodie. Although Mary Annette isn't that bad."

"Unless you say it too fast," I pointed out.

"I'm just lucky I ended up as Bonnie Lynn and not Bonnie Blue," Bonnie said. "Mama was rereading *Gone With the Wind* when she was pregnant with me. I might have been Melanie."

"Now there are Ashleys by the dozen, and they're all girls," Mam said. "A few Rhetts, too. Why is it that Rhetta sounds country and Rhett sounds more sophisticated?"

"It's because our cousin Junior Hill's wife is Rhetta, and she's about as country as they come," I said. "Well, so is Junior, for that matter. But what do you expect when your Christian name is Junior?"

"Did you know they named their baby Junior?" Mam asked.

"Oh, go on," Bonnie said. "They did not. What do they call him, Junior Junior?"

"Yep," Mam said. "And now Rhetta calls her husband Junior Senior. Honest. I'm not kidding."

"Junior Junior and Junior Senior." I shook my head. The dog formerly known as Pablo was lying contentedly in the sun, mouthing an old tennis ball. "No wonder some Yankees think we're dumb as dirt, and eat it, too."

"They're ones to talk. Some of those Yankee names can be pretty bad," Bonnie said. "You know, all Pilgrimy. Abigail and Priscilla are okay, but how would you like to be Prudence?"

"There was a Prudence Pinckney," Mam said.

"Really?" I cast my mind back over Miss Augusta's ancestors. "I don't remember her."

"I didn't either," Mam said. "But she's in Bradford's book, in that chapter on the Chathams. I saw her name before Bonnie Lynn here"—she shoved up against Bonnie—"started knocking over the furniture."

Bonnie shoved back, and I almost fell off the step. "Hey, watch it." Doc looked up. "It's okay," I told him. "Enjoy Chloe's tennis ball. I'll get you some of Jack's when we go over to Mama's." I turned to Mam and Bonnie. "How could there be a Prudence Pinckney in with the Chathams? Are you sure you read it right?"

"Pretty sure," Mam said. "We can go look. The disk's still in the computer."

Doc and Chloe came in with us. I gave them both a treat. "Look how smart he is," I said. "Sit, Doc." He sat. "Now, shake." Up came the paw.

"Now you have to give him another treat," Mam said.

"What a good boy Doc is. He's such a good dog." I fondled his ears. "Good Doc."

"Lindsey's in love," Bonnie said. "And this time with a real son of a bitch."

"Very funny," I said.

Doc thumped his tail on the floor.

"Here it is," Mam said. "Come look."

" 'Augusta was well looked after, first by Senator Chatham's niece, Elizabeth, and later by his own sister Letitia,' " Bonnie read aloud. "We read that already."

"No, here," Mam said. "Further down. 'Augusta Pinckney kept in touch with her Chatham relatives, especially her cousin Elizabeth, who ensured that Augusta attended the same boarding school that her mother, Edith, attended. Originally a finishing school for young ladies established before the Civil War, Briercliff was also where Prudence Pinckney had been educated. The youngest sister of Theophilus Pinckney of Indigo Island, she married James Chatham but died two days after the birth of their son, Robert.' "

"Theophilus—now there's a name for you—was Colonel Pinckney's father," Bonnie said. "The one Mam said was owner of Pinckney after the Civil War."

"And Robert Chatham was Edith's father," I said. "Which means she and Henry were either second or third cousins. I never can remember how that works."

"If that doesn't beat all," Mam said. She looked triumphant. "Miss Augusta *is* a Pinckney!"

chapter twenty

As the Tide Turns

"And so Miss Augusta is a Pinckney on her mother's side, if not her father's," I told Will.

"Wait," he said. "Let me see if I've got this straight. Henry Pinckney couldn't have been Miss Augusta's father because he was overseas when she was conceived, and Senator Chatham didn't want the scandal of a granddaughter born out of wedlock."

"Right," I said. "He probably pulled strings to cover up when Augusta was actually born. But his own mother was Prudence Pinckney. So Miss Augusta didn't have a motive to kill Bradford after all. As proud as she is of her family tree, she'd have known her parents were cousins and that there were Pinckneys on both sides."

"No, Lindsey, that dog won't hunt," Will said. "Although this one might." He looked at Doc, who was dozing on the living-room floor, his head on his paws. Doc had sounded like the hound of the Baskervilles when Will pushed the doorbell about ten minutes after I'd driven home from Mam's. But once I'd introduced him as my new alarm system, he'd sniffed Will thoroughly and settled down while Will and I çaught each other up on everything.

"What do you mean?" I asked. It all seemed logical to me.

"If Bradford had just told her about Henry not being her father, she might have been shocked enough to push him down the stairs, the way Pen claims." Will was sitting in Daddy's recliner, looking like a man who wanted nothing more than to lean back and go to sleep. He'd been up most of the night, first with the raid at Hillcrest, then interrogating Pen at the county lockup in Centerville.

"I wouldn't believe a word that self-serving little so-and-so says," I retorted. I was sprawled on the sofa with Peaches, who kept eyeing the dog like he was a creature from another planet. "Talk about two-faced! Okay, I can see where the news would come as a shock. And Miss Augusta, of all people, would hate for people to find out. She'd be ashamed, even though it's not her fault. Maybe they did have some sort of encounter in the attic, but Pen's your only witness. And as Bonnie said last night, who's going to take her word against a Pinckney's?"

Will looked thoughtful. He'd already told me Pen was still in jail, so far charged only with trespassing and assault. I hoped she was wearing an orange jumpsuit. The color wouldn't suit her.

"She has some wiggle room," he said. "I'm going to talk to her again this afternoon, as soon as her lawyer arrives." Once Will had said that the conch from Pinckney was at the crime lab and not at the bottom of the sea, Pen had clammed up, so to speak. Ironically, she'd had to call Bradford's lawyer to get the name of a criminal defense attorney. "We'll have to see if Miss Upchurch knows as much as she thinks she does about Bradford's activities on Indigo. Before she stopped talking, she said that she'd sold a few things from Indigo—some figurines, a snuffbox—through her antiques store for him. She thinks that incriminates Miss Augusta."

"Doesn't it?"

"Not necessarily," Will said. "Miss Augusta might have decided to sell a few things and asked Bradford to handle it. Or he could have pocketed them, saying he was having them restored or appraised. Just because he was blackmailing Pinck and Ray over Magnolia Cay and the slave cemetery doesn't mean he was blackmailing Miss Augusta, too."

"So he *was* blackmailing them!" I said. "I knew it! Did you get that from Jamie?"

"Yes," Will said. "I guess I can tell you that now. Jamie says they bought Bradford off with a deepwater lot and the promise of a share of the profits down the road, not that Ray or Pinck will ever admit it. They both have solid alibis, anyway. Don't think we didn't check. They were playing golf at Hilton Head with potential investors. Sally was squiring historical-society people around in the real-estate van, but Ray was miles away."

"What about Jamie?"

"Oh, he was awful quick to produce a gas receipt showing he was in Columbia," Will said. "Trouble was, he accidentally handed it to me with one from Cap's from the night you girls got shot at."

"I thought that was Eddie Smoak." I couldn't keep the surprise out of my voice. "You mean Jamie tried to kill us? I thought he liked us."

"He does like you," Will said. "But he overheard Mam telling Ray about the bone, and he thought he'd impress his dad and Ray by giving you a scare. 'Bout scared himself to death when he heard y'all go in the water. Thought he might have hit you. Turns out his aim's not as good as he thinks. I pointed out that his credit-card receipt from Columbia didn't have a time stamped on it, unlike that little slip you get from Cap's pumps. Then I confiscated his rifle. He was falling all over himself to confess to everything, so I'd believe he didn't kill Bradford." Will shook his head in disgust. "Not that he was a serious suspect anyway. No one reported seeing him at Pinckney that day, or anywhere near the island."

"That little twerp," I said. "I can't believe he was sober enough New Year's Eve to remember about the bone. I don't suppose you've heard anything about it yet."

"Actually, we did this morning," Will said. He yawned, then grinned apologetically. "Sorry. It's going to need some more tests, but yes, it is human."

"And is it old enough to be from the slave cemetery?"

"Well, that's the interesting part," Will said. "It appears to be much older. That's why there'll be more tests. The forensic anthropologists are excited. They think it could be hundreds of years old. Looks like Jimmy and Cissy may have found an Indian burial mound."

"Geez." I sat up. Peaches tumbled out of my lap, then moved to the sofa arm to stand sentinel. "Indians? Like in the Edistow tribe? Not a slave cemetery?"

"In all probability, that's there, too, or close by. The slaves may have heard legends that it was sacred ground, or discovered bones there as well. As to which Indians, there were a lot of small tribes in these parts before the colonists arrived. I expect Pinck's going to be hearing from archaeologists and scholars from all over wanting to do some excavations."

"Digging up the past," I said. I rattled the ice in my Coke. The power had come back on soon enough that I hadn't been forced to empty Mama's freezers and cart the contents to Mam's. "Of course, around here, you don't have to dig very far. The past is all around us. It's like Faulkner said, it's not even past yet."

Will looked at me. "You know, that's not necessarily a bad thing." His eyes held mine. "Lindsey, I don't want to be just a part of your past. I want to be part of your life now."

I didn't say anything.

"When are you coming back to Indigo?" he asked.

"Well, you might notice I haven't left yet." I smiled. "Mama and Daddy come back tomorrow, and they'll want to hear everything about a dozen times. I won't leave before Monday, and I expect I'll be back for a weekend in a couple of months—Easter, for sure. And I can always run down if you need me to testify or something. Will you?"

"I don't know," Will said. "Maybe. But that's not what I'm talking about. I'm talking about your coming back to stay."

"Stay?" My voice went up.

"Don't tell me you haven't thought about it. I know we haven't talked that much, but I know what I feel, and I think you feel the same way."

"Oh, really?" He sure was taking a lot for granted. "Will, you hardly know the first thing about me now. Or me about you, for that matter." He started to say something, but I kept going. "Yes, we were close once, but that was almost twenty years ago. We were both kids. I've changed, and I'm sure you've changed." I waved off his effort to butt in. Everything I'd been thinking and feeling the last week was spilling out. "Sure, there's been some chemistry, but we've been through some intense events. It's like when people get trapped in an elevator, or go through a hurricane together. You feel closer because of the experience. But it happens out of context, out of real time. You don't know if it's real."

"You finished?"

"No," I said. "What about Darlene? Y'all were married for a long time, and I'm not interested in getting involved in a rebound relationship. Been there, done that. And don't look so surprised. I haven't been sitting around nursing a broken heart for umpteen years."

"I didn't say you had," Will said. "All I'm saying is that I think we ought to give ourselves a chance to find out if this—us, whatever you want to call it—is real."

"But that doesn't mean I have to move back to Indigo, change my whole life just because you did," I said. "Why did you come back, anyway?"

Will looked weary. "At the time, I told myself it was because of Jimmy."

"Jimmy?"

"He should have graduated last year, but when Darlene moved out, he took it real hard. He started cutting classes and basically flunked his senior year. I thought it would be better for him to repeat it somewhere else, to have another chance."

"That sounds reasonable," I said.

"But I'd be lying if I said that was why I really came back." Will wasn't looking at me. He was gazing out the window, toward the dunes and ocean, the sand and sky. "All my life, I've tried to do the right thing, or at least what I thought was the right thing, what people expected of me. I took the scholarship to college even when the pro scouts were looking at me. Everybody said college was the smart choice, that I should get an education, that baseball could wait. You know what happened."

"Yes." He'd torn his shoulder up in a third-base collision junior year. It had healed, but his throwing arm was never as good as before—certainly not good enough for pro ball.

"Then there was Darlene. I wanted to break it off even before you and I got together. I tried a couple of times, but she'd cry, and I'd give in. And then that Christmas, I told her I really meant it. I didn't tell her I'd met someone else, but maybe she suspected. She didn't cry, said maybe it was for the best. And then, what, a month or six weeks later, I get this phone call. I should have called you, but I was a coward. And you were right when you said we were kids back then. I was until I got that phone call, and then I had to grow up real fast."

Will stood up. "I won't ever regret Jimmy—he's a great kid—and Darlene and I were happy for a long time. We were so used to each other. I told myself that it was for the best, that you and I were just a fling. And when I heard you'd gotten married that summer, it seemed like I was right. I didn't even know you were divorced for a long time. By then, we were in Columbia, Jimmy was a baby, and I was with the sheriff."

He stopped and turned toward the window.

"I put law school on hold for so long that I never got around to it. I liked being a deputy, working up to being a detective. Darlene said I fell in love with the work, and maybe I did. I still like it. And the smart thing, the thing everybody told me to do, was to stay in Columbia. But then Uncle Horace decided to retire, and Griggs called and offered me the job on Indigo. And even though I said it would be good for Jimmy, I knew deep down I was doing it for me. For once, I wanted to do something because it was what I wanted, not what everyone else wanted for me. I wanted to come back here. I wanted to come home."

This was the most serious I'd ever heard Will. And I wasn't sure I was ready for it. I'd meant the things I'd said. Indigo was home base for me, but I'd had a push-me, pull-me relationship with the island for a long time. That was why I'd gone off to work at summer camps in the mountains when other students were jockeying for jobs at the beach. It was partly why I'd gone out of state to college, and to England on spring break. I liked it that Charlotte was five hours away—close enough for long weekend visits but too far for me to impulsively hit the road whenever I was at loose ends.

"Lindsey, I don't want to have any more regrets where you're concerned. If you want to come down a couple weekends, and I can come up to Charlotte some, we can see how it goes. But I know now this is where I belong."

"Will, I—"

"You don't have to say anything now. We're both tired."

"Bone tired." I smiled.

"Just promise me that you'll think about it. And promise me one more thing."

"What's that?"

"Actually, two things. Let's see if we can keep the cousins and everybody else out of this for the time being."

"I'm all for that," I said. "But I would like to see you before I leave. I happen to be free tonight. After that . . ." I spread my hands.

He nodded. "I know. It'll get harder, with the family. I'll be back at eight, how's that? And I'll try not to fall asleep on you."

"It's a deal. But what's the other promise?"

Will walked over to me and took my hand to pull me off the sofa. "Support your local sheriff. Stay away from the FBI."

A stiff wind off the ocean rattled the palmetto fronds as I went to the CR-V to drive out to Pinckney. The tide had turned. The Dixie Chicks' *Home* CD started up when I turned the ignition. I'd forgotten to take it out earlier. Now, I wondered if it was some sort of sign. Could you go home again?

Bonnie was going to drop off Aunt Cora on her way to the airport so she could get her Olds, and Mam needed a ride home because Cora was going on to Miss Maudie's. I'd started to ask Mam why she couldn't drive her own car, and why she was even going to Pinckney at all, but then I stopped myself. It was easier to just say yes then to get into some long conversation that would no doubt touch on everything from cold pills to family nicknames and would end up with me still driving out to Pinckney. Besides, as Mam pointed out, I'd get to give Bonnie a proper good-bye.

I'd also have to tell them about the bone. Will had filled them in on Pen earlier, when he'd called Mam's looking for me. He'd also reported that Beth's spiced tea was just that. I'd let him talk to J. T. about Jamie before discussing it with Mam.

I sang along to "Landslide." I'd been a teenager when Stevie Nicks and Fleetwood Mac had sung it the first time. I'd liked it then, but now the words meant something.

I punched in the gate code and drove slowly up the drive. The shadows were lengthening as the afternoon drifted toward the brief twilight of winter. Mam and Bonnie were sitting on the porch steps, sheltered from the wind that whipped the moss and bent the boughs of the pines. Leaves skittered across the brick path.

"Y'all need some hoop skirts," I said. "In Pinckney purple."

"I think not," Bonnie said. "That's going to be your department."

"What are you talking about?"

"Mam will tell you."

In fact, Margaret Ann looked like the cat that swallowed the canary.

"Out with it," I ordered.

"We've been talking," Mam started.

"No, leave me out of this," Bonnie said. "Margaret Ann has been talking—to Pinck, to Beth, to Aunt Cora, to Miss Maudie. Have I forgotten anybody?"

"No, that's it," Mam said. "So far. Miss Augusta's in a coma. The tests show she's had a little 'brain event'—which I guess is doctor talk for a stroke. Pinck said the doctors told him that even when she wakes up—which could be days, weeks, maybe even longer—she's going to have a long recovery period."

"But she is going to recover?" I asked. "If not, we may never know what really happened in the attic."

"If she doesn't have a big 'brain event' or a heart attack or get pneumonia, she should get better," Mam said. "As to what she'll remember . . . They're bringing in all sorts of specialists. Pinck sounded hopeful." She patted the step beside her. "Sit down. Why didn't you bring Doc Pablo?"

"Stop calling him that," I said. I sat down so Mam was sandwiched between me and Bonnie. "His name's Doc. And I want him and Peaches to get used to being alone together, 'cause when I get home to Charlotte, they'll be spending most of the day like that."

"He doesn't look like a city dog," Mam said. "Don't you think he looks like a country dog, Bonnie? An island dog?"

"If you're telling me he looks like a trailer-park dog, it's only when he flattens his ears and lets his tail go limp," I said. "Personally, I think he's very handsome."

"He's a good-looking dog," Bonnie said, "and I'm sure he'll be just fine wherever he lives."

"He's living in Charlotte with me," I said. "Mam, if this is your way of telling me you want my dog, you can't have him."

"I have a dog," she said. "Nobody's trying to take your dog. No, I'm talking about you coming back to live on Indigo."

Wait a minute. I just had this conversation. Had Will conspired with them to get me to stay? No, he'd said not to tell them.

"Pinck has power of attorney," Mam said, "and he wants to hire you."

"Me?"

"He wanted me first," Mam admitted. "But I convinced him you'd be better."

"To do what?"

"To oversee Pinckney Plantation," she said. "Don't look so flabbergasted. It's a domino thing. Beth's going to be interim director of the historical society, which is what she wanted in the first place, and she and Aunt Cora are going to finish the photo book. But she can't run the historical museum and the Pinckney gift shop and plan Sue Beth's wedding, so I'm going to do the gift shop, because I can handle both it and Coming Up Roses. But someone still needs to do the stuff Miss Augusta did—coordinate events and tour groups, schedule and train the guides, oversee things in general. I'll help you in the beginning."

"I know nothing about running a plantation," I said. "Bonnie, tell her I'm not qualified."

"But you are," Bonnie said. "You were the waterfront director and then the senior counselor at Camp Pineloch in college. And you managed that bookstore for a while."

"That was years ago, and the bookstore went out of business." Although that hadn't been my fault. The times and the economy had done it in, like so many of its kind.

"We might have inflated your experience to Pinck just a tad," Bonnie conceded. "But you know a lot of history, you know Pinckney, and you're good talking with people."

"Not as good as Mam," I said. "She's the talker and the organizer."

"But you can be just as bossy," said Mam. "And you have more, more, um . . ."

"Tact?" I said. "Could that be the word you're searching for?"

"I just believe in saying things directly," Mam said. "Y'know, I call 'em like I see 'em."

"Girls, girls," Bonnie said. "Tell her the best part."

"It's only part-time—thirty hours a week—but it pays pretty well," Mam said. "And it'll have benefits and health insurance."

"You're kidding," I said.

"No, really," Mam said. "We convinced Pinck that if he wanted to keep Pinckney up and running, which he does, he needs to pay a good salary. And you could still write for *Perfect Pet* or freelance other stuff. You might actually come out ahead."

My mind was racing. Since ad revenues were down, Andrew probably would love for me to just freelance. And I had a duplex where the rent was about to go sky-high, thanks to the replumbing.

"Wait, wait, wait," I said. "I have no place to live. I'm not moving back in with Mama and Daddy. And I'm not moving in with you, Mam."

"I'm not asking you to," she said. "You tell her, Bonnie."

"Miss Maudie's decided to spend the winter with her son in Centerville," Bonnie said. "She wants you to stay at Middle House rent-free, just pay the utilities. You love Middle House."

"What about the summer? That's when you can't find anything affordable to rent on the island."

Already, reality was intruding. Did I really want to move back to Indigo, where everybody always knew everybody else's business? Was Indigo big enough for me, Margaret Ann, Mama, Aunt Boodie, and Aunt Cora? Would Will see this as an indication that I'd taken his words to heart and wanted a serious relationship? Was I willing to drive an hour to get to a movie or the mall?

"We'll figure something out by summer," Mam said. "If worst comes to worst, you could probably live at Pinckney."

"I don't know about that," I said. We might have solved the mystery of the ghost of Pinckney, but the place still felt haunted. How could it not, on this past-haunted plot of land? I hadn't even told them yet about the Indian burial mound. It was all too much. "I'll have to think about this, and I'm too tired to think about it now," I said. "I'll think about it tomorrow."

I looked down the shadowed drive, more conscious than ever of the old house behind me as a place where phantoms lingered—the spirits of planters, of slaves, of soldiers in dusty uniforms, yes, even of those stereotypical girls in hoop skirts and ringlets. They'd all been here before me, real people with needs and wants, hopes and dreams. All were gone now—but somehow not gone. "I'll think about it tomorrow," I repeated.

" 'After all,' " said Bonnie, her accent thickening, " 'tomorrow is another day.' " She fluttered her eyelashes.

Mam's head was bobbing in agreement. She stood up between

us and raised one hand skyward. "One thing's for sure, Lindsey," she said. "As God is my witness, if you come back to Indigo, you'll never go hungry again!"

epilogue

On the coldest night of the year, moonlight spills through the attic windows of the old house. The elongated shadow of a dressmaker's dummy stretches toward a corner, where a cage crouches in the darkness.

A clear night. A calm night. But not a completely silent one. The bough of an old tree scrapes against weathered wood; a dead branch taps at a leaded pane; a board creaks, as if drawing in from the cold.

A shadow shifts in the gloom. There's the small groan of an ancient hinge. A door opens.

The air stirs, bringing with it the faint tang of the sea, a whisper of frost. A dragging sound. The clink of old metal. Shuffling footsteps.

The house seems to hold its breath. Then the hinge creaks again. The door shuts.

All is quiet. For now.

acknowledgments

Fiddle Dee Death is a work of fiction. You won't find Pinckney Plantation, Indigo Island, or Granville County on any map of the South Carolina Low Country. Like the characters in the book, they are products of our imaginations. Where actual place names occur in the narrative, they have been used fictitiously.

Many family members and friends helped us in the writing of "the book." We would especially like to thank our parents, Frances and Donald Pate and Boodie and Robert Godwin; first readers Kathy Hogan Trocheck and Mary Ann Horne; the Edisto Island Historical Society; Joan Fort of Seaside Plantation; Boone Hall Plantation; Nancy's colleagues at the *Orlando Sentinel*; Ron Sikes and Men with Mortgages; Katy Miller; Ed Malles; Nancy Lassiter; Detective Eric Hampton of the Alachua County Sheriff's Office; Detective Donny Kennard of the Sarasota County Sheriff's Office; and the entire staff of John F. Blair, Publisher.

CAROLINE COUSINS is a pseudonym for Nancy Pate and her "one-and-a-half-times" first cousins, sisters Meg Herndon and Gail Greer. (Their mothers are sisters, and thier fathers are first cousins.) Nancy, book critic for the *Orlando Sentinel*, lives in Orlando, Florida. Meg, a former elementary-school teacher, and Gail, a floral designer and former plantation tour guide, live in Mount Pleasant, South Carolina.